Matt's forty, possibly too late to change his life around, but his age isn't going to stop him. He has a chance at a new life for himself and his daughter with the Rosewood pack and intends to make the most out of it. Apparently, that includes playing bodyguard during a mission to save a new friend's brother.

Tyler has been in a cage for years and doubts he'll ever get out of it permanently. When he's bought during the auction, he's not surprised. What does surprise him is when his mate, of all people, is the one who gets him out of that cage and out of the infernal hell his life has been for over a decade.

Tyler is finally free, but he doesn't know what to do with his life beyond being with his mate. Matt offers him everything he's ever wanted, but it comes with a complication—Matt's ex-wife, who is also the woman who's kept Tyler prisoner.

Pamela is dangerous, but so is Tyler, and he's not afraid to use his strength and his gargoyle form to defend his new family.

The Gargoyle's Heart
Copyright © 2023 Catherine Lievens
ISBN: 978-1-4874-3949-1
Cover art by Angela Waters

Published by eXtasy Books Inc

Look for us online at:
www.eXtasybooks.com

THE GARGOYLE'S HEART
LEGENDARY SHIFTERS 10

BY

CATHERINE LIEVENS

CHAPTER ONE

Matt had no idea what he was doing. He really shouldn't be here, especially since he had a daughter at home, but a part of him needed to do this.

The other part was scared shitless.

"Do I really have to wear this?" Angus asked. He was looking down at himself.

Obviously Angus didn't like what he was wearing, but Matt knew that wouldn't stop him from going to the auction to rescue Ryland's brother, Pembroke.

"I tried to convince Remi to let you wear a t-shirt, but he nixed the idea," Ryland told him.

Ryland was wearing a suit that looked like it cost more than Matt had ever earned in a month. It probably did, too, especially considering the suit Ryland had bought for Matt. Matt had tried to convince him he didn't need something that expensive just to play his bodyguard for one night, but Ryland had ignored him. Remi, Ryland's best friend, would be wearing something similar, and they needed to look alike if they wanted people to believe they were both there to protect Ryland.

So here was Matt, wearing an expensive black suit and a white shirt, about to go to a fucking auction where people were bought and sold and act like Ryland's bodyguard even though he'd never hurt a fly. Why was he doing this again?

He glanced at Angus, who looked like he wanted to hide. Considering what he was wearing, it was understandable. The pair of loose pants and the vest were close to transparent and didn't hide much. It made Matt uncomfortable, and he wasn't even the one who had to wear it.

"Ryland already has bodyguards. That's not why you're there," Remi, Ryland's friend, said.

"I know we're hoping people will presume what my role is in Ryland's life, but do I really have to expose so much skin? I feel ridiculous. I can't believe the other shifters there will be dressed the same way."

"Some of them will. Some will wear even less. If this is too hard for you to deal with, you need to tell us now."

This was why Matt had volunteered to participate. He'd wanted to be there for his son Del and his son's mate Angus, but he also wanted to help these people being sold. No one should ever be treated that way, and he was appalled to know it was happening so close to the home he'd found with the Rosewood pack. He also wanted to prevent his son from going, because that wouldn't have ended well. Del wanted to protect his mate, but he was too involved. If anyone looked at Angus the wrong way, Del wouldn't hesitate to attack, and he'd ruin the work they were doing tonight.

"You don't have to go if you don't feel up for it," Del said from where he was watching Angus.

He didn't look happy about what Angus was wearing, but probably no-one in the room was. They didn't want Angus to be vulnerable, but this was the plan, and they needed to stick to it.

Angus looked straight at Del. "I'll do it."

Del looked like he'd wanted Angus to change his mind, but Matt could have told him his mate wouldn't. Angus was convinced of what he was doing and would go through with it.

Matt peered down at the black suit he was wearing. Part of him wanted to take Angus's place, but another part was happy that he wouldn't have to wear those ridiculously transparent clothes.

"If everyone is ready, we should head out," Remi said, breaking the tension rising in Cam's office.

Matt was relieved but didn't miss his son's glare. Del's heart was in the right place, and he wanted nothing more than to protect his mate, which was one of the reasons he needed to stay back. Having him there with Angus would end in a disaster, and Matt kept that in mind as he told himself he could do this.

He wasn't sure about that, but now wasn't the time to change his mind. He'd already volunteered and agreed, and he'd go through with it, even though he'd never done anything like it.

Contrary to everyone around him, he was human. He'd lose if he had to fight a shifter, but that wouldn't stop him from trying. These people had become his family, even though he'd been with the pack for such a short time, and he'd protect them. He'd especially protect Angus, Del's mate and future. Angus was why Matt had volunteered and why he nodded at Remi's suggestion that they leave, then followed him out of the office.

Matt didn't miss the fact that Angus was the last one to leave the room or that Del was back there with him. He decided they needed a few minutes, so he followed the others outside of the house and toward the car waiting for them.

"You feel ready for this?" Mercer asked.

Mercer was Ryland's other fake bodyguard, and Matt felt a certain kinship with him, even though he probably shouldn't. Mercer wasn't human. To be honest, Matt wasn't quite sure what he was, even though he suspected Mercer was a shifter. He'd trained Matt for a few days once Matt had volunteered for the job, and he'd kicked Matt's ass more times than Matt had been able to keep count. He wanted Matt to be ready for whatever might happen during the auction, and even though Matt had hated him a little every time he kicked him down, he was also grateful.

"I don't think I'll ever feel ready for anything like this, but I'll do it," Matt told him.

Mercer nodded. "That's all we can ask for. I don't expect there to be a fight since we'll be there under false pretenses, but we need to be ready for anything. If Ryland's brother is there, we have to be able to get him out, and that might bring a fight to us."

"I'll fight if I have to." But Matt really hoped he wouldn't. He wasn't a fighter, and his children were the only thing he'd ever fought for.

Which was what he was doing tonight.

Matt stared at the limousine parked in front of the house. He'd never been in a car like that, but having to do so tonight didn't make him happy, considering what they were planning. He squared his shoulders and straightened his back, telling himself to stop thinking about not knowing what to do and focus on what he knew he *could* do. He could fight. Mercer had shown him that when they trained together. He could be there for Angus, be his father-in-law, and protect him as best as he could. He'd be Angus's support tonight, since they'd decided Del should wait in the car rather than attend the auction with them. Angus was part of his family now, and Matt's entire being would be ready to protect him if anything happened.

He followed Ryland and Angus toward the limousine. He was glad Mercer would be driving, and he slid into the passenger seat in the front, closing the door behind himself. The window that separated the front from the back was open, so he could hear what Ryland and Angus were saying.

"You'll be fine," Ryland told Angus. "Even if Mercer and Matt are busy, I can protect you. I did create a private security company, after all."

Which meant he was probably better at this than Matt.

What the fuck was Matt doing here? Protecting Angus and making sure Del didn't do anything stupid. That was all he had to focus on.

"My safety isn't what I'm worried about," Angus said.

"It's not the only thing I'm worried about, either."

Silence descended in the car after that. Matt was pretty sure they were all thinking about what they'd find once they arrived at the auction. They were in this to save Ryland's brother, but they didn't even know if he'd be there tonight. What they did know was that it wouldn't be easy for them to go through this without freaking out. Remi had warned them that they couldn't save every person they saw tonight but that they'd be tempted to do just that.

Matt believed him. He only had to imagine the situation they were about to walk into to know he'd want to save every shifter auctioned. The problem was that it might ruin their possibility of finding Ryland's brother, which wasn't something any of them wanted to consider. Hopefully, once they had him back, they could focus on the people who'd hurt him and countless others and free everyone they'd have to leave behind tonight.

Matt wasn't sure if he was relieved or even more anxious by the time they reached their destination. He stared at the gray building in front of them, knowing what was happening inside but having a hard time believing it. It looked so boring from the outside, but it was evil on the inside. He was sure of that, even though he had no idea what they were walking in on.

But he was about to find out.

Tyler should be used to this by now, but he wasn't sure he ever would be. A part of him still rebelled at the thought that he was being bought and sold like a piece of meat. A bigger part of him had given up trying to fight it, so he allowed the people around him to order him around and do whatever they wanted with him. It was less painful, at least physically.

He'd been going from bad situation to bad situation since he'd been fifteen, and this wasn't anything he hadn't already lived through. He'd been sold and bought several times, but things had improved after meeting Pembroke. They'd been friends and had supported each other through every auction, every insult, and every slap.

But Pembroke was gone. He'd been sold, and Tyler would never see him again. He had to remember that and stop thinking about his best friend.

That was easier said than done.

"All of you need to be ready in ten minutes," a voice snapped.

Tyler looked down at himself. He was only wearing a tiny pair of white shorts, and half of his ass cheeks hung out. A few years ago, he wouldn't have been caught dead wearing this, and he still had to resist the urge to cover his chest with his arms. He knew better than to do that.

But some of the people around him didn't. One of the other guys whimpered and tried to wrap his arms around himself, and the guard walking past him slapped him on the back of the head. The man sobbed but dropped his arms, and the guard nodded, clearly satisfied.

But he wasn't the guy in charge. The person in charge wasn't even a guy.

The sound of heels striking the floor made Tyler shiver. He kept his gaze on the ground, not wanting to see the woman who'd hurt him so badly. She'd never touched him, but she didn't need to.

"What a sight all of you are," she said, a hint of purr in her voice. "You'll earn me a lot of money tonight. Behave, and everything will be all right for everyone."

Tyler was pretty sure that was a lie, but he kept his mouth shut. The guy from before was still crying, and he heard Pamela walk toward him. He tensed, already knowing what would come.

Pamela wasn't physical. As far as Tyler knew, she'd never hurt any of the people she and the man she worked with had sold or bought. She didn't need to.

"Stop crying," she snapped.

The sound of crying stopped.

"That's better, but you need to wash your face before going out there. I can't sell you in this condition. Now, I need you to start smiling and not stop until you're out of this building. Can you do that for me?"

Tyler risked a glance upward. The man who'd been crying was nodding at Pamela, who wore a bright red dress tonight. It went well with her red lipstick, but Tyler thought it made her look like she'd been drinking blood. She wasn't a vampire, but she was a monster, so he supposed anything was possible.

She snapped her fingers. "Give him a dose," she ordered one of the guards. "I can't have him freak out on stage."

The man whimpered again, but he didn't try to fight. Like everyone else in the room, he knew it was useless.

The drugs were one of the reasons Tyler had stopped fighting. Every time he came back here, he saw new people, and usually, they'd been drugged. Pamela and the others needed their merchandise to be calm and appeal to the buyers, and that wasn't going to happen if they were sobbing or screaming. He'd stopped behaving that way because he didn't want to be drugged. In the beginning, he'd thought that he could use the fact that he wasn't drugged to his advantage, maybe to escape. But there was no escaping Pamela and the people she worked with, and he'd given up trying a while ago. Maybe he'd have a chance if he got bought tonight, but he wasn't even sure he wanted to try. He didn't have anything or anyone out there.

"It's time," Pamela declared. "Make me proud, all of you, and earn me a lot of money. I need a new dress."

A surge of hate made Tyler need to grit his teeth. He couldn't do something as stupid as telling Pamela to fuck off or, worse, attack her. She wouldn't hurt him tonight, but if no one bought him, she'd make sure he knew what she thought of his behavior.

So instead of doing what he wanted, he got in line and followed the guards out of the room. He shivered as the air around him became warmer. Where they'd been before was all cement and cold water for their showers, but now they were in the area where the buyers spent time. They needed to be kept comfortable, so it was warm enough that Tyler wasn't cold anymore.

He and the others were made to stop on the side of the stage. Tyler could hear Fulton talking to the buyers, introducing himself and explaining what was about to happen. Tyler didn't need to listen to him to know. He'd been through this too many times. He hadn't been sold often, and his entire body hurt at the memories of what had happened to him when he had been.

He didn't know if he wanted to stay back or if he wanted to be sold. Some days, he thought it was better for him to stay here because he already knew the people who worked the auctions. He knew which were the cruelest, which didn't care, and not knowing what he'd find if he was bought was a more frightening prospect—one he didn't want to think about.

"Programs with the names and details of the shifters about to go on auction are being distributed right now," Fulton said. "Please, take a few minutes to go over them and make your choice. I hope everyone will find something they want and will enjoy. Although, of course, the only way to win who you want is by using your credit card."

Some of the people in the room laughed, and it made Tyler want to scream. Instead, he pressed his lips together and kept his gaze downward.

Then things started moving. He wasn't the first in line and didn't pay attention to what was happening. He couldn't afford to. He'd cared about Pembroke, and when his friend had been taken away, it had hurt so badly that he'd told himself he wouldn't go through that again. He couldn't afford to make friends or care about the other people being sold.

"Now this one is special," Fulton said.

Someone pushed Tyler forward, and he knew his time had come.

"I know by looking at him and seeing how small he is, you'd never think it, but Tyler here is a gargoyle shifter."

Tyler stepped onto the stage. He went straight to the middle of it, standing to face the crowd. He couldn't see them, because the room was dark and there was a spotlight on him, but he didn't have to see them to know what was about to happen.

"Let's start with a hundred thousand dollars," Fulton said.

Tyler idly listened as the people he couldn't see tried to outbid each other. He didn't pay much attention until someone loudly said, "Five hundred thousand dollars."

Tyler blinked but kept his gaze down, knowing nothing good could come out of this. Whoever this person was, they really wanted him, and when that happened, it never ended well for him.

"I don't think I recognize that voice," Fulton said.

"You don't have to recognize it," the man trying to buy Tyler snapped. "Is the shifter mine?"

"We'll find out soon enough. Does someone offer five hundred fifty thousand dollars?" Fulton asked with a chuckle.

No one answered, and Tyler's stomach dropped.

He'd been bought.

Matt had resisted the urge to jump onto the stage too many times to keep count. He didn't think he'd ever been so pissed, not even when Pamela had dumped Cora into his arms and vanished without even asking about her sons. He'd given up hope that she cared a long time ago.

But the anger he felt now burned and made him want to do something stupid. Clearly he wasn't the only one feeling that way, because Ryland had just bought one of the shifters put on auction.

"Tyler is yours, mysterious buyer," Fulton said with a smile.

Matt wanted to strangle the smile off the man's face. Fulton was slimy and evil, and Matt hated being in the same room. At least Tyler was nowhere near Matt and Angus.

Tyler was ushered off the stage, and another man was pushed onto it. Matt looked away, unable to continue facing the reality Remi had warned him and the others about. He wished he could rescue all these people, and while it was good that Ryland had saved at least one of them, too many had been sold.

"Remi is going to be pissed," Angus murmured.

Ryland didn't answer. He stared straight ahead as the auction continued, then, as soon as it was over, he got to his feet. The problem was that none of them knew what to do. Pembroke hadn't been auctioned, so they still didn't know where he was, and now, they had a new probably terrified gargoyle shifter to get out of here before anyone realized what was going on.

Before they could leave the balcony, the curtain behind them opened, and Fulton appeared. Matt gritted his teeth and stayed behind Ryland, his expression as smooth as possible even though he wanted to kill the guy.

"A new face," Fulton drawled as he stopped in front of Ryland.

He ignored Mercer and Matt, for which Matt was grateful. He wasn't sure he'd have been able not to look disgusted if Fulton had paid attention to him.

The problem was that after staring at Ryland, Fulton turned his attention to Angus, who stood next to Ryland. Angus stared at the floor, playing the role of a frightened pet, and Matt wondered if he was afraid. Matt certainly was, and he hadn't drawn the attention of the dickhead auctioneer. He'd pull Angus behind him if he could, but he knew better than to ruin this chance.

"Where can I retrieve my purchase?" Ryland said before Fulton could do something stupid like trying to touch Angus.

He even placed himself in front of Angus, which helped Matt feel less like he needed to step in. He had no doubt that Fulton wouldn't have taken it well if a mere bodyguard had dared intervene.

Fulton looked slightly uneasy, but he chuckled. "Eager?"

"I paid half a million dollars for him, so yes. I'd like to take him home."

"And skip dinner?"

Ryland looked like he wouldn't hesitate to punch Fulton if he didn't tell him where to go. Matt almost volunteered to hold Fulton while Ryland beat the shit out of him, which wasn't like him. What was happening to him?

"I didn't come here to have dinner with people I don't know and couldn't care less about," Ryland said, sounding like he truly didn't care. "I came here for the shifters, and now that I have one, I'm ready to head out."

"I can assure you that the food is perfect, as is the company. Most buyers stay to talk to other like-minded people, and business connections are often formed. Besides, if you're planning to attend more of my parties, maybe it would be good for you to get to know the others."

Matt wanted to scream. He had no doubt that Ryland was a big dollar sign to Fulton, which would explain why he was trying to get him to stay. He couldn't read Ryland's expression, or maybe he didn't care. Either way, Fulton wasn't letting go, and Matt found himself ready to step forward.

"Take me to Tyler," Ryland ordered. He leaned closer to Fulton, and for the first time, Fulton didn't look so smug and smarmy. He almost looked scared, and while he quickly schooled his expression, Matt had seen it, and it was highly satisfying.

"Now," Ryland continued. "I'll pick up my purchase and head out. If you want to talk about business, you're welcome to contact my company."

"Should I invite you to my next party?"

"Only if you have something interesting to sell."

Ryland reached back to take Angus's hand. He pushed past Fulton, who quickly stepped aside to avoid being mowed down. Matt almost expected him to continue pushing for Ryland to stay for dinner, but thankfully, he had more sense than that.

"Take him to the cages and hand him his purchase," he told one of the bodyguards waiting for him in the hallway. "I'll see you soon, Mr. Young."

Matt prayed he wouldn't have to see Fulton ever again as he walked past him. Mercer was tense next to Matt as if he expected something to happen, but they made it out into the hallway without any problem. From there, they followed the bodyguard who was taking them to Tyler. They left the area of the auction and the plush balconies behind and entered a cold hallway through a door. Everything here was cement and easily cleaned, which made Matt shudder. It was too easy to imagine what had to be cleaned off this floor.

Matt had thought it was hard while they were still in the hallway, but it was nothing compared to what they found when the bodyguard opened a door at the end of the hallway. They walked in, and Matt realized that while he'd thought he hated Fulton before, it was nothing next to the burning need to kill the guy he felt now.

Two rows of cages lined the walls. Some were empty, but most contained the shifters who'd just been auctioned. They still wore the tiny white scraps of clothing they'd had on during the auction, and Matt knew they had to be cold, but he was pretty sure the cold was nothing next to the fear they had to be feeling. They all pressed at the back of their cages, as if it would save them from being taken out and handed off to the people who'd bought them.

Tyler wasn't an exception. He stared at their group with wide eyes from the back of his cage. The door was open, but he didn't try to escape, and Matt understood why. He couldn't have gone anywhere. There were guards standing by the two doors Matt could see, and they looked like they wouldn't hesitate to use force to get the shifters to stay in their cages and obey orders.

The group stopped in front of the cage, and Matt couldn't look away. He didn't want to move and do something stupid, so he hung back like any other bodyguard would have, even though he wanted nothing more than to reach for Tyler. He didn't understand why, but he supposed he was a protector at heart. Tyler wasn't one of Matt's kids, but he was small and frightened, and that was enough for Matt to want to take care of him.

Angus stepped toward the cage. He didn't go in, but he reached for Tyler with a hand, then waited for Tyler to make the next move. For a moment, nothing happened, and Angus and Tyler stared at each other.

Matt held his breath until Tyler finally moved. He took

Angus's hand and allowed him to pull him out of the cage. He was still only wearing the tiny pair of white shorts he'd had on during the auction, and Matt could see goosebumps on his skin, so he quickly took off his jacket. He hesitated, not wanting to spook Tyler, but the man was cold, so he draped the jacket over his shoulders, taking care not to touch him.

Tyler looked back at him, and Matt expected him to move away, but instead, his eyes widened as he stared. They were close enough to touch, and Matt could smell the shampoo on Tyler's hair. He wanted to be closer, so he put a hand on Tyler's shoulder, relieved when Tyler didn't freak out.

Tyler had a long road ahead of him, but he wasn't alone anymore, even though he didn't know it yet.

Tyler had been fearful when the door opened after he'd barely managed to get into his cage. Everyone knew what it meant after an auction.

Usually, the people who bought the shifters waited until after dinner to pick them up, but not always. This was one of those times, and Tyler's luck meant that they were here for him. He'd watched the small group, wondering which of the men had bought him. It didn't matter, though.

Not when one of them was his mate.

Tyler found himself leaning back against the hand on his shoulder and taking a deep breath, inhaling his mate's scent. It was all over the jacket his mate had given him, and Tyler wondered if he'd be allowed to keep it. He wanted to, but it looked and felt expensive, and he didn't see why his mate would allow him to do so.

Tyler didn't know what to do. He'd never met his mate, and the fact that the man was part of the group who'd bought him made Tyler wonder what would happen next. Mates were supposed to love each other, but Tyler couldn't be sure that was what would happen. If his mate was with a man who didn't hesitate to buy shifters against their will, what did that mean? Was he okay with what happened at the auction, or did he hate it and was only here because his boss had dragged him along?

Tyler had many questions, and he could ask none of them. The guards surrounding him and the others wouldn't hesitate to hurt him if he was rude, and that wasn't something he wanted to deal with at the moment — or ever, really. This was his chance to make it out, and he'd do anything to escape.

Tyler held his breath as they made their way through the building. They'd never let a buyer leave through the back door, which meant that Tyler was allowed to move through the area reserved for the buyers. He'd seen it before, and it made his stomach churn. These people sat in luxury, eating and laughing, while Tyler and the others suffered in their cages.

But Tyler wasn't in a cage anymore. He didn't know what would happen to him, but he'd find out soon enough. No one had yelled at him for now, and no one was hurting him. That was more than he could have hoped for, and he prayed things wouldn't change as soon as they were out of the building.

His heart raced as he finally stepped out, leaving the guards behind. He took a deep breath of night air, cleaning his lungs from everything he'd had to breathe through until now. He expected someone to push him forward, but instead, they waited for him, as if they cared about what he was going through and how he felt. He didn't understand it, but he quickly nodded, and when they started moving again, he wasn't surprised to see they were guiding him toward a limousine.

Tyler's mate quickly moved around him to open the limousine's back door. He wasn't the first one to slide in. The man who did wore the most expensive suit of the bunch. He was probably the one who'd bought Tyler. He certainly seemed to have enough money.

The man wearing the ridiculous transparent clothing was next. Tyler had thought he might be a pet, like Tyler, but he didn't behave that way. That made Tyler wary, but he didn't have a choice. He had to follow them inside the car, and he did so, tightening the jacket he'd been given around his body.

Tyler squeaked when two strong arms wrapped around him. His mate gently pushed him into the car, climbing in with him and keeping him close. Tyler's eyes widened when he saw two men waiting inside the car. He waited for them to do or say something, but one was too busy kissing the man Tyler thought wasn't a pet even though he was dressed like one. The man with the expensive suit wasn't saying anything about his pet kissing someone else, and Tyler wondered what was happening. Who were these people? Why had they bought him?

Where were they taking him?

"Let's go home," the man with the expensive suit said.

One of the bodyguards who'd been with him inside had gotten into the driver's seat, and he nodded. He'd already started driving away, for which Tyler was grateful. He didn't want to spend one more second in that place and hoped he'd never have to return. He wouldn't be the one making that decision, though. His new buyer would, and Tyler looked around the car again, wondering which one it was. It *had* to be the man wearing the expensive suit.

"I'm Angus," the man with the transparent clothing said. He was still cuddled into the other man's arms. "And this is Del, my mate."

Tyler didn't know what to do, so he kept his mouth shut. Usually, that was what was expected of him.

"And I'm Ryland," the man with the expensive suit said. "I'm sorry about all of this, but we needed to get out before they realized something was wrong."

Tyler had known something was happening since Angus had offered him his hand, but he was too afraid to hope. There was no way these people wanted to free him. After all, Ryland had bought him.

But the situation was nothing like what Tyler was used to. That was enough to give him hope, and he prayed he wouldn't be wrong.

"And these are Doyle, Matt, and Mercer," Angus continued, pointing at the other men in the car.

That was how Tyler learned that his mate's name was Matt. From what Tyler could smell, Matt was human, but that was okay. He didn't care what his mate was, just that he had one and that said mate was protecting him. Matt hadn't let go of him since they'd sat in the car, and he hadn't given any sign that he was going to. He was still hugging Tyler, and Tyler didn't hesitate to snuggle deeper against him.

He didn't miss the way Del and Doyle looked at each other, but he didn't care. He just wanted a moment of happiness in his mate's arms first.

No one said anything else. They knew Tyler's name, since they'd been at the auction and had bought him, and they seemed happy to give him space, for which he was grateful. He was confused and could feel exhaustion pulling him toward sleep. He never slept well in his cage because something could happen at any second, but he wasn't in his cage anymore. He was in his mate's arms, and even though he didn't know what it meant or what would happen, he felt safe for the first time since he was fifteen.

Unfortunately, it didn't last long. Eventually, the limousine stopped, and the doors opened. Tyler tensed, knowing he'd arrived at his new home. What would Ryland expect from him? Angus clearly wasn't Ryland's pet, and while Tyler didn't understand why they'd faked it, he wasn't about to ask.

He just wondered if he was supposed to be warming Ryland's bed or if Ryland had bought him for another reason. He was afraid to find out, and he clung to Matt as they got out of the car.

Tyler looked around, desperate to find his footing. The place was nothing like he'd expected. Considering everything, he'd thought Ryland would live in an expensive mansion surrounded by a security system, guards, and maybe even dogs. Instead, the car had stopped in front of a decently sized house that appeared to be in the middle of a forest. The only things Tyler could see as he glanced at the area were trees and several other small houses with their lights off.

Two men stood in front of the house. They came closer, and Tyler took a step back, but Matt was there. He smiled at Tyler and gently pushed forward, and Tyler could only go along with it. He wanted to please his mate, even though Matt didn't know what they were to each other since he was human.

"This is Toby and Cam. Cam is the alpha of this pack, and Toby is his mate. They'll take care of you. You're safe now, and while I know you can't believe it, I promise that no one will hurt you."

Tyler didn't want to leave Matt, but he didn't dare say out loud that they were mates. So he had to allow Toby to guide him away, but he looked back until Matt wasn't visible anymore. He desperately wanted to go to him, but instead, he followed Toby deeper inside the house, still wondering what was about to happen to him.

CHAPTER TWO

When Matt woke up the next day, everything that had happened during the auction felt like a dream. It hadn't been like him to go and do what he'd done, and he couldn't quite reconcile it with what he knew about himself. He didn't regret going and helping Tyler, but he did regret the fact that they hadn't found anything about Pembroke. Pembroke was the reason they'd gone, yet Ryland still had no idea what had happened to his brother and where he was.

Matt stared at the ceiling for a moment, listening to the quiet of the house. Cora still seemed to be asleep, something he'd take advantage of. These days, she wasn't happy if she wasn't awake at five in the morning. It felt like a small miracle that it was six thirty and he hadn't heard anything from her. It also made him wary because the saying that silence was dangerous was true when it came to his daughter, but he could take a few minutes to bask in the sensation of being in a comfortable and warm bed, safe and happy.

For a while, he hadn't believed he could have this. After he lost his job, everything had been so hard. The only reason he hadn't drowned in despair was his children, and he'd never be able to thank his sons enough. Doyle especially had put himself in danger and had done something stupid just to help the family. It had ended well, but the thought of what could have happened to him still made Matt sick to his stomach when he thought about it.

So he didn't, at least not this morning. Doyle was safe and sound in his mate's arms, as was Del. Matt didn't have to worry about either of them or Cora. She was safe, too, and soon she'd wake up and demand breakfast. Matt would be busy, which meant he needed to take advantage of this moment of peace.

His thoughts drifted straight to Tyler. Matt couldn't help but wonder how he was and whether he'd slept. It had to be scary for him to be in a new place surrounded by people he didn't know, especially after what he'd lived through. From what Matt knew, no one had given him an explanation last night, which meant Tyler probably believed Ryland had bought him because he wanted something from him. The thought of what that something could be made Matt shiver, and he pulled the sheet tighter around his body.

What had happened to Tyler? What had been done to him? It wasn't a question Matt was about to ask because it was Tyler's story to tell, but he wanted to help the other man. He didn't understand why and honestly didn't care why he felt that way. It was probably because his sons were all grown up and didn't need him anymore, and while Cora was only six, she was becoming more independent every day. Matt didn't want Tyler to be dependent on him, but he wanted to feel useful. He wanted to help, and he had no idea how to do that.

The sound of a door opening made him smile. Right now, he'd have to focus on his family, and that was perfectly fine. Cora deserved all the attention, at least until she went to school.

Matt got up and met his daughter in the hallway. Her hair was all over the place, and she was rubbing her eyes, still half asleep. He gently kissed the top of her head before guiding her toward the bathroom. He'd have to brush her hair again after she was done, but in the meantime, he went to her bedroom, put some clothes on her bed so she could get dressed, and headed downstairs to get breakfast ready. By the time she appeared in the kitchen, she looked more awake, but her hair hadn't changed much. She'd attempted to brush it, but only on one side, which made Matt smile.

"I missed you last night," she said, coming closer to hug Matt.

"I missed you, too, but I returned late and didn't want to wake you."

"Is your friend okay?"

Matt had told her that he and the others were going to help a friend. He didn't want to lie to her, but she was only six and wouldn't have understood the situation. Besides, Matt intended to shield her from the worst of the world for as long as he could. "We didn't find him. I'm sure he'll be fine, though."

She nodded, trusting him implicitly. It always made him want to hug her. Instead, he gestured toward the table so she'd sit down and eat.

While she did that, he went back upstairs to set her bedroom back to rights and opened the windows. He kept an ear open, but everything was quiet downstairs, only the sounds of cartoons reaching him. Cora was a calm child, unlike her brothers. She didn't usually need a lot of supervision, which made Matt feel a bit useless. That probably meant it was time for him to find something else to do. He'd been wanting to get a job since he and Cora had arrived in Rosewood, but the last time he'd mentioned it to Cam, the alpha had waved him off and told him to focus on his family. Matt had done exactly that, and it had done wonders for all of them, but with Doyle and Del settled with their mates, Matt needed more.

His cell phone rang while he was going home from taking Cora to school. He liked that the school in Rosewood was much smaller than the one Cora had gone to in the city. She already had a few best friends, and she didn't cry when he left her there anymore. He was proud of her for becoming more confident, but it also made him feel odd to know that his daughter had an entire life during the day that didn't include him. First grade was an adventure, and she was dealing with it like a champ.

Matt was surprised to see that the alpha was calling him. It no doubt had to do with last night, and while there wasn't much Matt would be able to add to what Ryland, Mercer, and Angus could tell Cam, he was more than happy to give his report.

"Hello?"

"Hi, sorry to bother you so early. I hope I didn't wake you up."

Matt chuckled. "No fear of that. I just took Cora to school."

"I didn't think about it. It's clear I'm not a father."

"What do you need from me?" Matt was eager to help.

"As I'm sure you can guess, we're having a meeting this morning. I went over the footage of the camera Ryland had on, so I know what happened, but it wouldn't hurt to have a chat."

"I can certainly come, but I doubt I can tell you anything different from Mercer and Ryland. We were never separated."

"That's fine. You were there, so I'd like you to be present at the meeting. Besides, I suspect Tyler will be more comfortable if you are."

"How is he? Did he get through the night okay?"

"I haven't seen him yet. He was understandably wary and afraid yesterday, so anything we can do to make him more comfortable will be welcome. He seemed to be more relaxed with you around, which is why I think it would be good for you to be present."

"I'll be right there."

Matt had been part of this mission, part of the group who'd gone out to save Pembroke. They hadn't found him, but they'd saved Tyler, and even if that was the only good thing that came out of that mission, Matt would be proud of it.

He knew several people in the pack were working on this daily, like Doyle's mate. He was a rare shifter, and he'd been hunted. He'd even been kidnapped because someone wanted to put him on auction like they had with Tyler. The thought of what happened to these rare shifters when someone grabbed them made Matt want to hit something, and he wasn't a violent man. He hated that some people felt they could treat rare shifters like that. Those people weren't animals. They might be able to turn into one, but that didn't change the fact that they were human and deserved as much respect and love as anyone else. Instead, they were treated like objects and like they didn't matter, and while there wasn't much Matt could do about that, he *could* make Tyler feel like he was so much more than what he'd been treated as.

As long as Tyler was okay with Matt's presence, Matt would be there. It might only be a transfer from his sons needing him to Tyler, but that was all right. Matt was still trying to figure things out. He'd only been in Rosewood for a short amount of time, and he was still trying to find his footing. Maybe helping Tyler would help him, too.

Tyler wasn't sure what to do when a knock came on his door. He stared at it from the bed where he was still curled up, wondering who it was and what they wanted from him.

So far, no one had demanded he do anything. After Toby had shown him this room last night, he'd left, and Tyler hadn't seen anyone else. He hadn't believed he was truly safe in the beginning, and he still wasn't entirely sure, but the bedroom door had a lock on it, and he'd used it. Then he'd taken the longest shower he could remember taking, and he'd felt better once he'd gone back to the bedroom. He'd found clothes in the drawers of the dresser and put on a pair of sweatpants and a t-shirt. He'd slept in those, hugging one of his pillows, terrified that something would happen during the night.

Nothing had. He'd woken up because he hadn't thought of pulling the curtains, and the sun had hit him in the face. He'd spent the time since then curled up in bed, looking around the bedroom and out the window. The only thing he could see out there were trees, and he wanted to explore, but there was no way he was leaving his bedroom. He felt almost as safe as he'd felt in Matt's arms yesterday.

He sat up. Maybe it was Matt. Maybe he was back for Tyler.

There was another knock, and Tyler hopped out of bed. He quickly finger-combed his hair, hoping it hadn't dried weirdly, and went to crack open the door.

It wasn't Matt.

Tyler stared at Angus, wondering what he was doing here. He was dressed normally this morning, and he looked more comfortable.

"Hi. I don't know if you remember me from last night, but my name is Angus."

Tyler almost rolled his eyes. Instead, he opened the door just a bit more. "You were with the man who bought me." And Tyler had so many questions about that. Where was Ryland? Why had he bought him only to leave him with Toby and Cam? What did he expect from Tyler?

"I was. How are you feeling?"

"Confused." That word described how Tyler felt at the moment perfectly.

For some reason, it made Angus smile. "I would be, too, if I were in your shoes. Do you want to come with me to the kitchen? We're having a meeting over what happened last night, and we'd like your input."

Tyler wanted to say no and stay in the bedroom. The only

reason he didn't right away was that maybe Matt would be in the kitchen. He'd been there last night, so surely, he'd be present at this meeting. Tyler needed to be sure. "Will he be there?"

"Ryland will be there, but even though he bought you, he's not a bad person. He just wanted to help you."

That wasn't what Tyler had been asking, although he understood why Angus had thought so. Still, what Angus was saying about Ryland didn't convince Tyler. He'd been through this too many times. "That's what they all say, but he's not who I was talking about. He's a bodyguard. Will he be there?"

"They're both already there."

That was enough for Tyler. Now that he knew that his mate was in the house, he felt braver, or at least brave enough to leave the bedroom and face this meeting. He swallowed and squared his shoulders, eager to see Matt.

How would Matt react? He still didn't know that he was Tyler's mate, and Tyler didn't know if he should tell him. Would Matt get angry to find out he was linked to a shifter like him? Besides, Tyler didn't know anything about Matt. He might be married or have a partner. Tyler couldn't just dump the fact that they were mates in Matt's lap and expect everything to be all right.

"Everyone here wants to protect you, including Ryland," Angus said, instead of taking Tyler to Matt. "I know we didn't tell you much yesterday, but you'll learn more during the meeting. Just know that Ryland's brother was kidnapped, and he's been looking for him ever since. I think you remind him of him. That's why he bought you, but you're free, even though he paid a lot of money for you."

Tyler nodded. He wasn't surprised that Angus was trying to reassure him, but he didn't trust him. Right now, he didn't trust anyone except maybe Matt, but he wasn't quite sure about that just yet. Maybe if he could see Matt, he'd find out if he could trust his mate.

Thankfully, he didn't have to prompt Angus. The man guided him through the house toward a room from which he could hear several voices. Tyler smelled coffee and food, and his stomach rumbled. Angus shot him a smile, but as soon as Tyler walked into the kitchen, his gaze found Matt.

He wasn't wearing a suit today. Instead, he wore jeans and a sweater and looked comfortable leaning against the counter. Tyler didn't even think about it. He went straight to his mate, needing his presence to feel better. He grabbed the edge of Matt's sweater and tightened his hand around it, wanting to be sure his mate wouldn't disappear.

He had expected Matt to push him away or ask him what was wrong with him, but he didn't. Instead, he smiled gently. "How are you this morning?"

Tyler had no idea how to answer that question, so he shrugged. He didn't care how this looked to everyone else in the kitchen. He only cared about Matt, and he had him back after wondering if he ever would for most of the night. Everything else could wait.

He was given food and ate it, still clinging to Matt, who said nothing about it. Tyler never wanted to let go, so he was relieved when Matt didn't ask him to, even after they moved the meeting to Cam's office.

"So, what did we find out yesterday?" the alpha asked after sitting down behind his desk. "Apart from the fact that some people are monsters."

"I cloned Colbert's phone," Angus said.

Tyler wondered what that meant. He knew the meaning of the word cloning, but he hadn't gone to school since he was fifteen and hadn't had access to technology for most of his life. He'd missed a lot, and while that didn't mean he was stupid, it made him feel like he was because he didn't fully understand a lot of what was said around him. Maybe if he focused instead of obsessing over Matt, things would be better, so he tried to do that.

"Is there anything about my brother on there?" Ryland asked once Angus was done explaining what he was planning on doing with the phone.

"Not that I was able to find, but I'm sure that if your brother was auctioned by these people, I'll find his name. Pembroke isn't common, after all."

Tyler sucked in a breath at the sound of his best friend's name. Everyone in the room turned to look at him, which made him want to hide behind Matt. Since Matt was still standing, he moved behind him, and while he didn't manage to hide completely, he felt better.

"Tyler?" Ryland asked.

Ryland was the man who'd bought Tyler, which meant Tyler didn't trust him. He wanted to, and he remembered that Pembroke had talked a lot about his brother, but Tyler wasn't sure he could trust anyone.

"Tyler?" Matt asked, slightly twisting. "Do you recognize that name?"

It was Matt who was asking, and Tyler found himself answering. "He's my friend."

"Can you tell me about Pembroke?"

Tyler ignored the wounded sound coming from Ryland and focused on Matt instead. He was afraid they were going to take him away if he didn't give them what they wanted. He didn't think Matt would allow that to happen, but that didn't mean these people wouldn't become violent. Tyler didn't know them. He didn't know anything about them.

But so far, they hadn't hurt him, and if they were truly trying to find Pembroke, he wanted to help them. He missed his best friend and needed to know what had happened to him.

"We were together," he whispered. "He's my best friend,

and we lived together for a long time. But when our owner died, we were given to the people who sold me last night." Tyler hadn't been sorry for their owner, but he'd been terrified and sad because he and Pembroke had been separated. "Pembroke was sold before me, and I haven't seen him since. I don't know where he is now."

"Do you know who bought him?"

"A man called Colbert. I heard him boast about it." And he'd seen that Colbert guy take Pembroke from the cage after the auction. Both he and Pembroke had been crying, and Tyler had begged Colbert not to take his friend.

The asshole had laughed. That was the last memory Tyler had of Pembroke and of the man who'd bought him. He wanted to hurt Colbert for that.

And maybe he'd have the occasion to do it.

Matt's heart broke a little every time Tyler opened his mouth. He wanted to find this Colbert guy and hurt him like he'd hurt Tyler, even though he wasn't a fighter. His emotions were all over the place, which wasn't something that usually happened. He didn't quite know how to behave, but he did know that his focus had to be Tyler.

"We need to go now," Ryland said, already getting to his feet.

"We can't," Cam interjected.

"You told me you'd help me get my brother back." Ryland started pacing the length of the office.

Ryland wasn't a shifter, but he reminded Matt of a tiger stuck in a cage. He'd finally found out something about his brother. Matt wasn't sure how close they were to getting Pembroke back, but at least they knew who had bought him, and they had the man's cloned phone. It was more than they'd expected to get and more than they'd had yesterday.

"I will," Cam promised. "We all will."

"Then why are we talking about this? We should already be out there, headed toward this guy's house."

Tyler pressed closer to Matt, and Matt reached back for him. He wrapped an arm around him to keep him close, knowing that Tyler needed the contact. It didn't matter that Matt didn't understand why Tyler was clinging to him. He just wanted Tyler to be okay.

He didn't seem to be at the moment. He trembled against Matt's back, probably because of the way Ryland was reacting to the news that they weren't rescuing his brother yet. Matt didn't blame Ryland, but he didn't like the fact that Tyler was terrified.

"We can't just barge in there," Remi said, clearly trying to soothe his friend.

But there was no soothing Ryland. "Why not?" he snapped.

"Because someone could get hurt."

"I don't care if I get hurt. I only care about Pembroke."

"What if the person who gets hurt is him?"

Matt was glad Remi said that. Considering what Matt had seen yesterday and the kind of person who would buy another human being, it was too easy to imagine that Pembroke had been hurt since he'd been bought. It was also easy to think that the man who'd bought him wouldn't hesitate to get rid of him if it meant getting rid of Ryland.

"Remi is right," Cam said. "If I had my way, I'd go right now. I don't want anyone to be in Pembroke's position for a second longer than strictly necessary. It's not exactly the same, but my mate was a prisoner for a long time."

Tyler shuddered again, and Matt turned a little to look at him. It wasn't easy because Tyler had buried his face against Matt's sweater, but Matt needed to be sure he was all right. "You're safe here," he whispered.

Tyler peered up at him. "I trust you, but not these people."

Matt wasn't surprised. "You might not trust them, but I do. I trust them with my family, and they're the most precious thing I have in the world. I'm not asking you to trust anyone here, but since you trust me, maybe you can at least try?"

Tyler turned his attention back to the rest of the room. They were all focused on Angus, who was talking back to Ryland. They weren't fighting, even though their voices, especially Ryland's, were loud.

"Let *me* do my job," Angus was saying. "I understand you want to help your brother right away. I do, too, especially after seeing what we saw last night. But we have no idea what we'd walk into, and I don't know about you, but I have no doubt that shifters are guarding the place. You never told us what kind of shifter your brother is, just that he's a rare shifter. What would Colbert use him for?"

"He's a hydra shifter."

Matt blinked, trying to remember what a hydra was. He'd heard the name but wasn't a shifter expert. Thankfully, he didn't seem to be the only one who wasn't sure what to expect when it came to Pembroke.

"That's the dragon with three heads, right?" Angus asked.

"I don't know if I'd call him a dragon, but you get the idea, yes."

"Is it true that his heads grow again if they're cut off?"

Ryland didn't look happy over the way the conversation was going, which Matt could understand. He wanted to do something, to act and get his brother back, and instead, he was stuck here. It had to be frustrating, and Matt could only imagine how he felt. He didn't have any contact with his siblings, but it seemed that Ryland cared about his brother almost more like a father than a brother, which Matt understood all too easily.

In the end, they all decided it would be better to wait to go get Pembroke. Angus needed to go through the phone he'd cloned, and hopefully, he'd find more information about Pembroke and where he was being kept. Ryland wasn't happy, but he wasn't working alone, so he had to agree with the plan. Unfortunately, there was nothing anyone could do at the moment except wait. Everything was in the hands of Angus and Everly. They were the computer experts, so hopefully, by the time they were done, they'd be able to go out there and get Pembroke.

Matt was already invested in finding Pembroke before because he could understand how much it had to hurt Ryland not to have his brother, but now he wanted to give Tyler his friend back. He probably wouldn't be involved in the mission, but that didn't matter.

Matt noticed Del coming toward him. He wasn't surprised, and he suspected his son would have come sooner if they hadn't been in a meeting. He probably wanted to check in with Matt, make sure he was all right, and no doubt ask questions about Tyler and why he was clinging to Matt the way he was. Matt only had an answer to the first question, and he hoped Del would accept that. Matt's son could be stubborn when he wanted to be, which was most of the time when it came to family. He was protective of all of them, no doubt because of what had happened recently. Knowing that made Matt feel guilty, but Del was an adult, and he was capable of shouldering the negative aspects of the world. Matt had to remember that.

Matt felt Tyler peek from behind him only to jerk back when he noticed Del. The movement had been enough to give Del pause, so Matt waved him closer. He didn't know if Tyler would be part of his life in the long run, but if so, he'd have to get used to having Matt's family around. So he turned and wrapped an arm around Tyler's shoulders, pulling him forward. Tyler looked slightly panicky, but Matt quickly explained who Del was.

"This is Del. He's my son, and you don't have to be afraid of him."

Tyler stared at Del for a moment while Matt held his breath. He didn't know why it was so important to him that Tyler and Del got along. Tyler probably wouldn't stick around for long, but Matt already couldn't imagine his life without Tyler. It didn't make sense, and now wasn't the right time to focus on those feelings. He wouldn't be able to ignore them forever, but for today, he could.

"You were there last night," Tyler told Del.

"I was."

"Why?"

Del looked confused, but he answered. "Because my mate was there."

"You're a shifter's mate?"

Matt remembered Angus explaining this to Tyler last night, but it wasn't a surprise that Tyler didn't remember it. He'd been confused and afraid and probably couldn't remember much of what had happened. It was a good thing. Matt wouldn't want anyone to remember something like the auction, but especially not a sweet man like Tyler.

"I am."

"I didn't know that was possible." Tyler's voice was soft, and there was clearly something on his mind.

He glanced at Matt, and Matt smiled at him, hoping to reassure him. He didn't want Tyler to be afraid. He wanted Tyler to like it here in Rosewood and to decide to stay.

Tyler had known Matt was his mate since they'd met, but he hadn't thought they could actually be together. He wasn't sure why except maybe for the fact that he'd never seen a human and a shifter together.

Most of the humans he'd dealt with in his life were people who thought they were better than shifters. They'd never stoop so low as to be in a relationship with one, even when they had sex with them. Sex was completely different from relationships, and Tyler had learned that a long time ago. He wanted sex with Matt, of course, but he also wanted so much more.

Should he tell Matt they were mates? His son seemed happy to be Angus's mate, so maybe Matt wouldn't mind. But Matt had children, which meant that there'd been someone in his life at one point. Was that person still there? Was Matt going home to someone he loved every night?

Tyler didn't know, and he was afraid that telling Matt about their bond would change everything. He didn't want to hurt Matt or to lose whatever was between them, even though he didn't know what it was. Maybe it was nothing, or maybe their bond was already growing. Whatever the case, he had no idea what to do.

He turned to see Ryland coming toward them. His heart raced, and he could feel panic starting to take over. He was afraid of Ryland, but if it was just him, he thought he'd be okay. The problem was that Matt was here, and Tyler wouldn't allow Ryland to hurt him.

"It's good to see you're doing all right," Ryland said once he was close enough. He was smiling, but Tyler was panicking.

"Since you said you're my brother's best friend, I thought that maybe you'd like to come with me once this meeting ends," Ryland continued. "You can stay with me until you decide what to do."

Tyler needed to protect his mate and himself, and there wasn't much he could do in his human form. So he shifted.

He barely took note of the shocked way people were looking at him before he grabbed Matt and pushed him behind his

33

back. Matt had done the same earlier, but it was Tyler's turn to protect him now. He wouldn't let anyone touch Matt, and he wouldn't let anyone take him away from his mate.

"Everyone stop," the alpha ordered.

To Tyler's surprise, they did, even Ryland. The man was human as far as Tyler knew, but he seemed to respect Cam, which made Tyler hope that maybe he wasn't dangerous. He was still the man who'd bought him, but he was also Pembroke's brother. Tyler supposed he should give him a chance, and he was willing to, but not if Matt was in danger.

Ryland raised his hands and quickly moved back as if he realized he'd done something wrong. Maybe he had. It didn't take a genius to understand that Tyler was freaking out.

"I apologize. I'm not sure what made Tyler react this way, but I mean no harm to him or Matt," Ryland explained.

"Ryland suggested that maybe Tyler wanted to go with him," Matt explained to the room. He put a hand on Tyler's shoulder but didn't try to move around him.

Tyler could have explained himself. Even though he was in his gargoyle form, he could speak. His voice was different than in his human form, but he was understandable. He didn't like that everyone was staring at him, though. That was the reaction he usually got when he shifted into this form, which was one of the reasons he tried not to. There was also the fact that the people who bought him had done so because they wanted a gargoyle shifter, and he didn't like giving them what they wanted.

Tyler was so much more than his gargoyle. He was a man, and right now, that man was terrified.

When Tyler felt Matt move, he panicked even more. He wrapped his wings around him, doing everything he could to keep him behind his body. It was the only way he knew for sure that Matt would be safe.

But Matt wouldn't stay back. Instead, he put a hand on

Tyler's arm and pushed away one of the wings. "Ryland wasn't trying to hurt you or me, and he won't take you away if it's not what you want," he explained.

"I just thought that since you said you were Pembroke's best friend, you might want to stay in his room until he comes back," Ryland interjected.

Tyler was still trying to make sense of the words. He understood them and their meaning, but the panic was still there. Ryland was trying to take him away from Matt.

"I'm not going to take you away," Ryland promised.

"You bought me," Tyler said.

Ryland's eyes widened at the sound of Tyler's voice. Tyler knew why. When he was in his human form, his voice was normal. In his gargoyle form, though, it was deep and guttural, perfectly paired with his stone body.

But even though Ryland appeared surprised, he didn't seem afraid. He faced Tyler head-on. "I did, and I'd do it again if it was necessary. I didn't buy you to hurt or use you, though. You reminded me of my brother, and I couldn't leave you there. I'm glad I bought you and brought you here, and I wish you'd believe me when I say I only want what's best for you."

"I don't want to go with you." Tyler needed Ryland to know that. He needed *everyone* to know that and be aware that if they tried to force him, he'd fight. He didn't know what kind of shifter most of these people were, but that didn't matter. He wouldn't allow any of them to take him away from his mate.

"Then you don't have to," Ryland said. "I'll be more than happy to help the pack financially support you until you get your feet under you. You're free now, Tyler. The fact that I bought you doesn't mean anything. It's not even legal."

Tyler almost snorted. "That's never stopped anyone." He'd been bought and sold several times, so he knew what some humans thought of him, and it was nothing like what Ryland was saying. Tyler wanted to believe the man, especially since he was Pembroke's brother, but could he? He'd been told too often that he was nothing more than a commodity and someone to be used. Very few people in his life had seen him as a person, and he didn't know where Ryland fell when it came to that.

Ryland nodded. "I realize that, and I hate that you had to live through that. You won't ever have to again if I have anything to say about it." He turned to look at Cam. "Can your pack keep him here? Will it be a problem?"

Cam instantly smiled at him, and Tyler was relieved he didn't have to wait for an answer.

"Of course not. Tyler, you're welcome to stay for as long as you want or need. You can even become a Rosewood pack member if that's what you wish."

Tyler frowned. Was Matt a pack member? It would make sense since he lived here, but he was human, and humans didn't have packs.

Tyler didn't understand how packs worked. He'd never been part of one or of any group of shifters. He didn't know what he was doing and was afraid to say the wrong thing. What if he agreed and became a pack member, and Matt left? But what if he said no, and Matt was a pack member and was disappointed?

"Is Matt a Rosewood pack member?" he asked because he needed to be sure.

"I am," Matt told him. "Not for very long, but my son found his mate here, and the entire family moved. It's our home now, and I'm not leaving. You don't have to, either."

The relief that flooded Tyler helped him relax, so much so that he ended up shifting back. He only ever used his gargoyle form when he was ordered to or when he was trying to protect himself or someone else, and clearly, the gargoyle didn't think he needed to be protected from anyone in this room. It gave him hope that these people truly only wanted the best for him.

This was all he'd ever wanted—a place to feel safe, someone who would love him and protect him. He didn't want to be bought and sold ever again. He wanted to live his life, fall in love, and build a family.

He burst into tears.

He hadn't been planning to do that, and he quickly scrubbed his eyes, but he couldn't stop the tears. Matt pulled him into his arms, hiding him from the others, and Tyler burrowed against him. He was overwhelmed and had no idea how to stop crying, but maybe he didn't have to.

"You can even move in with my family and me," Matt said as he rubbed Tyler's back.

Someone made a weird sound, but that didn't stop Matt, who continued, "Del is okay with it, and I can't imagine Cora will have anything to say against it."

That was enough for Tyler to look up. "Who's Cora? Is she your wife?"

"No. She's my daughter. I don't have a wife or anyone else in my life that way. You'd just be living with me, my son, and my daughter."

Matt wasn't married. He didn't have anyone in his life. This was more than Tyler could have hoped for, and for the first time in as long as he could remember, he found himself *wanting* to hope. He had everything he'd ever dreamed of so close that he could touch it.

"I'd like that. I'd like to be part of your family," he told Matt.

And that was all he needed to do to have everything he could ever want.

CHAPTER THREE

Matt pushed open the door and ushered Cora into the house. The smell of something cooking welcomed them, and Matt paused, briefly wondering who was cooking. It was still odd to remember that Tyler now lived with them, and he found himself smiling at the same time as he felt guilty.

Tyler shouldn't be cooking. He should be resting and relaxing, gathering his thoughts and deciding what he wanted to do with his life. That was why Matt had offered to have him live with his family, but it was as if Tyler needed to make himself useful, or rather, like he thought he had to.

"It smells good," Cora said, giving Matt a toothless smile. She'd lost two teeth in quick succession, and she'd been over the moon when the tooth fairy had visited her.

He smiled back. She was still so young, and a few dollars under her pillow was enough to make her happy. Things were so different with her than they were with Doyle and Del, but then, Matt's sons were adults. Del still officially lived with Matt, but he'd been spending most of his time with Angus, almost as if he felt he wasn't welcome. Matt had wondered if it was because of Tyler's presence, but Del had been quick to tell him that wasn't so when he'd brought it up. He and Angus had just recently gotten together and were making the most out of the honeymoon phase.

Matt straightened his shoes and Cora's, then took her hand and led her to the bathroom. He'd taught her that the first thing she needed to do when she arrived home was to wash her hands. He kept an eye on her to make sure she didn't just run them under the water for a second and call it a day, then took her place at the sink.

He could barely remember what it was like to have someone in his life. The only serious relationship he'd ever had was with Pamela, the children's mother. They'd been way too young when they had Doyle, still in high school. They'd stayed together, mostly for Doyle, then when Del had arrived, for him, too. Matt could never regret having his kids, but sometimes, he did wonder what his life would have been like if Pamela hadn't gotten pregnant. Then, he realized he wouldn't have his sons, and he decided his life was perfect just the way it was, especially recently.

Even more so since Tyler had become part of it.

Cora ran out of the bathroom and headed to the kitchen, no doubt to spy on what Tyler was doing. She was fascinated by him, something Matt easily understood. She could get away with staring at Tyler with adoring eyes, but he couldn't. If he tried, Tyler would probably tell him to fuck off and leave, which wasn't something Matt wanted to have happen. No, he wanted Tyler to feel at home with him and Cora. He wanted Tyler never to leave.

He still didn't know why he felt that way. He hadn't allowed himself to examine his feelings yet, but he would have to, eventually. It wasn't fair to him or Tyler not to, and Tyler already had more than enough unfair things to deal with. The last thing he needed was to have Matt drooling all over him if he didn't want it.

Matt washed his hands, then followed Cora to the kitchen. Like he'd expected, she was sitting at the counter, swinging her legs as she watched Tyler stirring something in a baking pan. He turned, and the smile that appeared on his face was almost enough to take Matt's breath away. It made Matt want to pull him into his arms, kiss the top of his head, and snuggle against him.

It shouldn't feel as natural as it did to have Tyler around, but it was as if he'd always been there, like he belonged. Matt had tried telling himself it was only because he'd been alone for so many years, but he wasn't sure that was it. He wanted to ask Tyler if he knew why he felt like that, but he didn't want to bother Tyler or send him running. So he kept the questions to himself, at least for now. That was another thing he and Tyler would eventually have to talk about, though.

"I thought I'd take care of dinner," Matt said.

"It's fine," Tyler murmured.

He always spoke softly, as if he was afraid Matt would snap at him if he didn't. It probably had to do with the way he was treated in the past, so Matt hadn't brought it up. As long as Tyler was comfortable, Matt didn't care, even if he never spoke.

"You're a guest, and you should be resting. It's my job to make dinner." It wasn't like Matt had anything better to do, anyway.

Tyler's smile disappeared. "I'm a guest," he repeated.

Matt could tell he'd said something wrong, but he wasn't sure why it was wrong. "For now, yes." He didn't want Tyler to be a guest. He wanted Tyler to be a permanent fixture in his life, but he was afraid to come on too strong. So he felt it was better if he cautiously poked to find out if Tyler would be interested in staying on a more permanent basis.

But how could Matt ask him to? He and Tyler weren't together. Matt was way too old for Tyler, and considering Tyler's trauma, Matt didn't feel he was a good fit for him. That hadn't stopped him from falling hopelessly in love with the man. Tyler was soft yet strong. He was incredibly resilient and sweet and a lovely and caring person. Matt didn't understand how anyone could not fall in love with him, let alone hurt him. The thought made him want to rage, even though he'd never been the violent type.

Tyler straightened his back. "Well, you went to pick up Cora from school and took her to her dance class. The least I could do was have dinner ready for the two of you when you returned. I thought you'd be tired."

Matt smiled at him. "I am, but it doesn't mean you need to do this every day."

Tyler had been. He kept telling Matt he enjoyed cooking, which was why Matt hadn't pushed too hard for him to stop. Everything Tyler made was delicious, so eating wasn't a hardship. But there was something more behind it, which was one reason Matt felt guilty about letting Tyler do all of this.

He looked at Cora. "Why don't you go shower? We'll eat as soon as you're done."

She wrinkled her nose. "But I'm hungry now."

"It needs a little more time in the oven," Tyler told her as he slid the pan back into the oven. "But as soon as you're out of the shower, it'll be ready."

Cora huffed, but she obeyed. Matt listened to her footsteps on the stairs for a moment, waiting for the sound of the bathroom door opening and closing. Then, he turned to Tyler. "I'm grateful for everything you do around the house," he said carefully. "And I'm extremely grateful for the food because it's delicious. I just need you to know that you don't have to do this and that I won't kick you out if you don't. I didn't ask you to move in with my family and me because I wanted a maid."

Tyler bit on his lower lip and looked down. "Why did you?"

That was easy to answer. "I wanted to give you a safe place where you could find yourself and heal. I don't know why, but you seem more at ease with me than anyone else. I hoped that having you in the house would help, but I'm not sure it is."

Tyler's gaze jerked up. "I don't want to leave."

"I'm not asking you to. You can stay for as long as you want. I just don't want you to feel obligated to do things."

Matt didn't expect Tyler to answer. Still, he waited, giving Tyler the time and space he'd need if he was going to.

"I need to be useful," Tyler whispered. "I'm scared that you'll tell me to leave if I'm not."

Matt wasn't happy about the fact that he was right. He also wasn't surprised, since he'd expected it, but he wasn't sure how to deal with it. The best thing would be for him and Tyler to talk, but they didn't have much time. Cora was hungry, which meant she'd rush through her shower to get back downstairs. Hopefully she'd at least rinse her hair properly, but Matt would have to go upstairs and check soon.

But first, he and Tyler needed to talk.

Tyler was sure he'd fucked up when Matt gestured at the chairs around the table. "Why don't you sit down and talk to me?" Matt suggested.

Tyler did sit down, but he pressed his lips together. What was he supposed to tell Matt? He'd already confessed why he was pushing to do most of the housework and cooking. It didn't matter that Matt had told him he didn't have to. The thought of not doing anything made Tyler panicky, and he didn't want Matt to kick him out.

He didn't think Matt would do it to be cruel like the other people had before. They'd bought Tyler and had thought of him as nothing more than an object. That wasn't so with Matt. He saw Tyler for the person he was, and he was clearly worried.

Tyler's hands shook as he sat on one of the chairs. Matt took the chair in front of him, and for a moment, they just sat there, the kitchen silent around them.

"It smells really good," Matt said, as if he didn't know how to broach the subject he clearly felt they needed to talk about.

"Thank you. I enjoy cooking and never had the opportunity to do so before. I'm having fun finding new recipes on the Internet and trying them."

Matt's smile came easily. "Good. I don't want you ever to have to do anything else that you don't want to do. That goes for cooking, the housework, or anything."

He leaned closer but didn't touch Tyler even though Tyler desperately wanted him to.

"I can't begin to imagine what you've gone through in your life," Matt continued. "What little I saw after the auction was enough to horrify me, and when I think about it, it makes me want to cry and find the people who hurt you at the same time. I'm not trying to tell you how to heal or what to do to feel safe. I just need you to know that I don't expect anything from you. As far as I'm concerned, if you want to spend the entire day in bed staring at the ceiling, you're welcome to do just that."

Tyler quickly shook his head. "That would be boring."

"I don't know. Sometimes, when Cora's at school, I do just that. I don't know how she can have that much energy so early in the morning, but I'm already exhausted by the time I'm back from the school run."

Tyler found himself smiling. He'd been living with Matt and Cora long enough to know how much Matt loved his daughter. The same went for his sons, but they were adults, so Matt's relationship with them was different. Matt adored Cora, and he was a good father to her, the kind of parent Tyler wished he'd had. If he had, he wouldn't have left home at fifteen, and he wouldn't have ended up being bought and sold and being hurt in ways he'd never thought possible.

"She does have a lot of energy," he agreed.

"And for some reason, she's taken a shine to you. I know she follows you around the house when she's home, but you can tell her to stop if you don't feel comfortable with it. I want you to feel like you belong here, Tyler. This is your home."

"But you said earlier that I was a guest." And being a guest meant that, eventually, Tyler would have to leave.

Matt sighed and leaned back in his chair. "I know what I said. Technically, I suppose you *are* a guest. I offered you to stay with Cora and me to give you a safe place to get your feet under you, but I'll be honest, it feels like you're part of the family. I understand it's ridiculous because we haven't known each other for long, but you belong here."

Tyler's heart raced. "Really?"

"Really. That's why I want you to know that you can stay for as long as you want, even if it's forever. This is your home, and Cora and I, along with Doyle and Del, are your family. You have to remember that. I don't know what happened with your biological parents or if you ever had anyone who cared about you, but you have us now."

Tyler licked his lips and wondered if he should tell Matt that they were mates. He wanted to, especially after what Matt had just said. His heart beat so hard it felt like it was about to jump out. He opened his mouth, but only a croak came out.

Apparently, the noise was enough to worry Matt because he got to his feet and walked around the table. He crouched next to Tyler's chair and put a hand on Tyler's thigh, his beautiful gray eyes making it obvious how worried he was.

"Tyler? Are you all right?"

Tyler couldn't get the words out. He wanted to tell Matt they were mates, but he was afraid he'd ruin everything.

Over the days since he'd arrived in Rosewood and moved in with Matt and Cora, he'd been trying to find his place in the house. He'd decided to do most of the chores and the cooking because he'd wanted to show Matt he could be useful and be part of the family, but he hadn't thought it would happen so fast, and now he didn't know how to deal with it. Technically, he was part of Matt's family because he was his mate, but Matt didn't know that.

How would he react if Tyler told him? Was he telling him all of this only because he felt sorry for him? Or was he telling the truth and could feel the bond between them even though he wasn't a shifter? The questions crowded Tyler's mind, and they made him want to run. He decided to follow his instincts, but they pushed him toward Matt instead of sending him out the door.

The kiss was quick, but it felt like coming home. Tyler's lips tingled when they met Matt's, and he found himself smiling just a bit. Matt's lips were a little rough but also gentle and sweet. Tyler pushed closer before realizing what he was doing. He'd even closed his eyes, and now, he opened them, panicking.

What had he been thinking? He hadn't even told Matt they were mates, yet here he was, kissing him as if he had the right to.

He stumbled out of his chair, needing to get away, not wanting to find out how Matt would react to the kiss. Before he could run out of the room, Matt's fingers wrapped around his wrist and kept him where he was. That made Tyler panic even more, even though he knew Matt would never hurt him. Matt was the only person Tyler trusted in the entire world.

"Wait," Matt said softly.

Tyler stopped trying to pull away. He'd have to face this eventually, so he might as well find out now what kind of mess he'd gotten himself into.

"Why did you do it?" Matt asked.

"I'm sorry. I shouldn't have," Tyler quickly said. He wanted Matt to know he realized he'd messed up.

Matt opened his mouth, but just then, Cora ran into the room, wearing her pajamas. Her hair was dripping wet, but she beamed at them. "I'm done," she declared.

Matt looked frustrated, but both he and Tyler knew he needed to focus on Cora. He let go of Tyler's wrist, and Tyler brought his arm close to his chest. Matt looked almost disappointed, but Tyler told himself that surely, he was reading his mate wrong.

He'd probably been about to berate Tyler for kissing him. He might have told Tyler he was welcome to stay for as long as he wanted and that he was part of the family, but Tyler suspected that he saw him almost like another son rather than a mate. It was partially Tyler's fault for not telling him they were mates, and he didn't know what would happen now that he'd made it clear that he didn't see Matt as a father.

For one, Tyler was too old to be Matt's son, even though Matt had his first son when he was still in high school. The bond was the most important thing, though. With that between them, Tyler would never be able to see Matt as anything but a mate, a man he was falling in love with and whom he wanted to share his life with.

"Let's go back upstairs," Matt told Cora.

"But I want to eat," Cora complained.

"You will as soon as you dry your hair."

She pouted but obeyed, and Tyler watched them leave the kitchen. For a second, he could imagine the three of them as a family. Then, he remembered that Cora had a mother and that he could never be another parent to her. He was too damaged to be a parent to anyone.

Matt ran Cora back to the kitchen as soon as they were done with her hair, but the moment between him and Tyler had been broken. When he and Cora walked back into the kitchen, the table was set, and Tyler was focused on the food. Matt tried to catch his eye, but Tyler firmly kept his gaze on what he was doing. Matt saw it for what it was. Tyler thought he'd made a mistake by kissing Matt, and now he was doing everything he could to act as if it had never happened. He probably expected Matt to behave the same way, and maybe that would be the smartest thing to do.

But Matt had never been a smart man.

In his place, most men would have tried to convince Pamela to get an abortion or give up their first baby for adoption. Matt had considered it. They both had, especially when Pamela's parents had told them they wouldn't support them if they decided to have the baby. Eventually, they'd decided to go ahead with the pregnancy, and Matt had never regretted it once in his life.

Things hadn't always been easy. In fact, they'd been difficult most of the time, especially after Pamela had left. She'd abandoned her sons, then later, her daughter. Matt would never be able to forgive her for that, but in hindsight, he suspected it was the best that could've happened. If she'd stayed, she would have come to resent the children, and they would have known.

It was also good that she'd known to bring Matt to Cora after she had her, even though she wasn't Matt's biological daughter. Matt didn't care about that. He'd raised Cora since she was a baby, and as far as he was concerned, she was his daughter as much as Del and Doyle were his sons. But not many men would have agreed to raise a child that wasn't theirs, especially with no mother in the picture. So maybe Matt was a fool.

If he was, he didn't mind.

Cora, Tyler, and Matt sat around the table, and Tyler placed a plate in front of Cora. She beamed at him, and he smiled back. The two of them shared a bond Matt hadn't expected. Watching them together made his chest squeeze to the point of pain. They looked like a father and daughter, and the three of them together looked like a family.

Matt wanted that. He and the kids *were* a family, but having another adult there, someone present for Matt, who would listen to him and help him, made everything different. Of course, things were still shaky because of what had happened to Tyler and the reason he was here, but Matt could imagine the three of them having dinner like this for years to come. He could see Tyler being another father to Cora, who'd only ever had one parent.

Tyler looked up, and his gaze crossed with Matt's. To Matt's surprise, he didn't look away. They stared at each other for a moment, and Matt thought they understood each other. He didn't know what would happen between them, but maybe if they were both willing to give this a chance, they could find happiness.

Tyler nodded and turned his attention to his plate. Matt picked up his fork, but he was still thinking.

Hoping.

After Pamela, he hadn't allowed anyone into his life and his heart. He hadn't been celibate since the boys had become old enough to be independent, but he'd never trusted anyone enough to bring them home and introduce them to his kids. Yet Tyler was here, having met all three of them. He lived with Matt and Cora, for fuck's sake. That meant that Matt trusted him, even though it didn't make sense.

Whatever Tyler had meant with that kiss, Matt wanted it. The problem was that he was terrified of fucking things up. His relationship with Pamela hadn't ended well, although it was probably as much Pamela's fault as it had been Matt's. Tyler was precious, and he'd already gone through too much in his life. Matt didn't want to cause him any more pain, so he was hesitant.

It wouldn't be enough to keep him away. He was a selfish man, especially after all these years of loneliness. Whatever

Tyler was willing to give him, he'd take. Maybe he and Tyler could heal each other and find a way to make this work, to become a real family.

And maybe Matt was getting ahead of himself, and Tyler had kissed him because he'd been overwhelmed and had needed comfort.

It was something Matt needed to consider, no matter how little he wanted to. He and Tyler would have to talk about it, but something told Matt it wouldn't be easy. When Tyler didn't want to talk about something, he made it his mission to avoid the person who wanted to talk to him. Matt didn't want Tyler to avoid him, but he had no doubt he'd have to hunt down the gargoyle shifter and corner him if he wanted to get to the bottom of this.

And he did. He wished to find out what the kiss had meant to Tyler and what Tyler wanted. He wanted to tell Tyler that he wanted him and be honest about how he might mess up sometimes because he had no idea what he was doing. He wanted them to learn how to be together and how to be a family.

Maybe the failed relationship between Matt and Pamela had been both their faults, but one thing Matt was sure of — Tyler couldn't be more different from Pamela if he tried, which gave Matt hope.

Over the years, Pamela had come to resent having a husband and two kids. She hadn't wanted to be held back and felt that was what they were doing. Maybe it was. As soon as the divorce was official, she'd left town, only returning once to leave Cora with Matt. That was six years ago, and Matt hadn't heard from her since then. He doubted he would, except if she had another kid, and he didn't want to consider that possibility. The thought was enough to make him shiver in horror.

So the fact that Tyler was nothing like Pamela was a good

thing. The problem might be something different. Tyler had been through things that very few people had. He'd need time and space to heal, and Matt wasn't sure how to help him deal with that. He didn't even know if there was anything he could do to help him.

For now, Tyler was still settling down with the pack and with Matt and Cora. Maybe Matt should talk to Cam to see if they could help Tyler in other ways, but it felt only right to talk to Tyler about it first.

That was if Tyler would allow him anywhere close after the kiss.

But Matt had a good reason to push. He wanted Tyler, even though it was probably foolish, and not just because of the age difference. So many things were working against them, but he found that he didn't care. As long as Tyler shared Matt's feelings, they'd find a way. Matt could see a future with Tyler and prayed that Tyler felt the same way. He didn't want to think about what would happen otherwise, so he didn't and focused on what was right in front of him instead.

Tyler and Cora were talking about the food Tyler had made. It was a concoction of chicken breast, cream cheese, and cherry tomatoes, and it was as delicious as it had smelled. Cora was even eating the tomatoes, which was a small miracle because she was in a no-vegetable phase. Matt was glad to see that Tyler was good with her, but he couldn't help but wonder if this was what Tyler wanted, too. Matt was pretty sure Tyler wanted him, but would he want the rest of the family? Would he want Cora, who was a package deal with Matt? Or would her presence be too much for him, considering how much healing he had to do?

Matt was afraid to find out the answer, but he'd ask the question. He had to.

Tyler could feel Matt watching him, but after the one time their gazes met, he carefully avoided looking up. It was best for him to focus on Cora, who was eating her food with an enthusiasm that warmed Tyler's heart. The recipe was simple—just chicken breasts, cream cheese, and cherry tomatoes, all dumped into the pan with salt, pepper, and oregano—but it was tasty, and Tyler liked that Cora was enjoying it so much.

Dinner was good, but eventually, it ended. Cora started wiggling in her seat, and since she was done eating, Matt told her she could go and play for a bit before brushing her teeth and going to bed. She shot off like an arrow, leaving Matt and Tyler alone.

Tyler got to his feet and started picking up the plates. He didn't know what to say, or even if he *should* say anything. He'd already apologized, but he was terrified that Matt would tell him it had been inappropriate or even kick him out.

Matt was a good person. He'd been there when Tyler needed him, and he'd opened his home and family to Tyler. And how had Tyler thanked him? He'd kissed him against his will, then had refused to talk about it. He'd fully understand if Matt decided this was over.

He could already feel the tears prickling his eyes, but he wouldn't push to stay if Matt wanted him gone.

"You don't have to do this," Matt said, getting up and taking the plate Tyler had been about to pick up.

Tyler froze. He needed to be useful. He needed *Matt* to see him as useful. "I'll just load everything into the dishwasher."

"You cooked. It's only right that I do it."

Tyler wanted to push, but he nodded and stepped away from the table. He expected Matt to bring up the kiss, but instead, he quietly started cleaning up the kitchen. Tyler wasn't sure what Matt expected from him, but he couldn't stay in the room for one second longer. So he left, heading straight for the porch.

He should probably go upstairs to his room and stay there for the rest of the night, but his skin was too tight. He felt like he was trapped. He realized he wasn't, but there was still a slight panic at the back of his mind, and he needed to get rid of it. He wouldn't be able to sleep otherwise.

He glanced at the dark forest, knowing what would take care of his restlessness. Apart from in Cam's office, it had been a long time since he'd last shifted and even longer since he'd allowed himself to spread his wings and enjoy the shift.

Shifters weren't just human. The animal or creature they could shift into was an integral part of them, and not being able to shift felt like missing a part of himself. He hadn't done it until now because he'd been safer in his human form, but he was free. He could do whatever he wanted, and no one would think badly of him or, even worse, try to use him. For the first time since he was fifteen, he could be himself.

He couldn't stop thinking about it now. He quickly took off his sweatpants and t-shirt, dumping them onto the bench by the front door. He didn't linger in his human form since he was naked except for his underwear. Matt and Cora were human, so they weren't used to seeing half-naked people walking around the way shifters were. Tyler's bits and pieces were hidden, but still. He didn't want to make anyone uncomfortable.

He allowed the shift to take over. He felt his body grow as he closed his eyes. His wings unfurled, and his skin hardened. It was almost as if he wasn't himself anymore for a few seconds. He was stronger and more capable of defending himself and the family he'd chosen. Maybe now that there wasn't someone to beat him down every time he tried standing up, he'd be able to do more.

But not tonight. Tonight, he could spread his wings and fly, which was what he did.

He pushed away from the porch as soon as the shift was over. His gargoyle form was massive, so he had to be careful not to break anything, but as soon as he was in the air, he found himself smiling like an idiot. He opened his arms and felt the wind on his skin.

Thankfully, his underwear was stretchy enough that he was still covered. They were a little tight, so he'd have to find another way to do this if he was going to shift more often, but for tonight, it was perfect.

He flew around the house a few times, looking at everything from another perspective. He hadn't left pack territory yet. He'd barely left Matt's house, but eventually, he would have to, and he wanted to know what was in the area. Luckily, as far as he could see, there were just a few houses, most of them hidden between the trees. Matt's house wasn't at the center of pack territory like Cam's. It had more privacy, which, as far as Tyler was concerned, was perfect.

He didn't fly far. He didn't think he could while knowing that Matt and Cora were in the house. Instead of heading toward town or exploring the forest, he found the sturdiest tree he could and sat up near the top, making sure the branch he was on could take his weight. As soon as he was sitting, he shifted to his human form and leaned back against the trunk.

Only to find himself face-to-face with a pigeon.

The pigeon was on a nearby branch, staring at him with its head cocked. Tyler tried to shoo it away, but the pigeon just sat there, staring, even when Tyler's fingers came so close that he could have touched it. It was odd, but he didn't think too much of it.

Until the pigeon shifted.

Tyler was ready to shift back to defend himself, but he was in pack territory. That meant he was safe, and since he knew he wasn't the only odd shifter who belonged with the Rosewood pack, he told his racing heart to give the pigeon a chance.

The pigeon turned into a man. In his human form, Tyler couldn't see much in the darkness, but he and the pigeon were close enough that he had a good view of the man, and the moonlight helped. He could see that the pigeon shifter had white-blond hair that fell in front of his face. He was small and thin, probably around Tyler's height, or maybe a few inches taller—which wasn't hard since Tyler was only five foot four.

The pigeon leaned closer, and Tyler watched him warily. What was he supposed to do? Should he say hello? He supposed he'd bothered the pigeon, but he hadn't realized the tree was already occupied.

"You're the new guy," the pigeon said.

"Unless someone else has arrived recently, I guess I am," Tyler confirmed. "I'm Tyler."

"Peregrine. Your gargoyle form is impressive."

"Thank you. And you're a pigeon?"

Peregrine snickered. He didn't seem to care that he was bare-ass naked sitting in a tree. Thankfully, it was the middle of the summer, so neither of them was cold. Still, the feeling of the bark under his naked ass couldn't be comfortable.

"Not a pigeon. I'm a caladrius shifter."

Tyler frowned. "I'm sorry, but I have no idea what that is."

"I'm not offended. I'm a rare shifter, so the fewer people know what I am, the better it is." Peregrine shrugged one shoulder. "Basically, I'm a bird shifter who can take away sickness and disperse it. I heal people."

Tyler's eyes went wide. He understood why Peregrine wanted to keep what he was and what he could do a secret. "I won't tell anyone."

"Thank you, but I didn't think you would." Peregrine grinned. "So, you're new, and I haven't been here long. What do you think about being friends?"

Tyler suspected he'd need a friend since the situation with Matt had gotten complicated. He didn't know if he could trust Peregrine, but at some point, he'd have to risk trusting someone. He already had with Matt, and it had been the right choice.

Hopefully, trusting Peregrine would be right, too.

CHAPTER FOUR

Matt was humming as he returned home from dropping Cora off at a friend's house. He'd decided it was time to talk to Tyler, who'd been avoiding him since he'd kissed him a few nights ago.

Matt understood why, and he didn't blame Tyler. He had to be overwhelmed. From the few things he'd said, he'd been in the hands of the auctioneers for years, probably most of his life. Even when he'd been sold, he'd always returned to them eventually. He hadn't had the opportunity to build a life or even think about what he might want. He was probably confused, which Matt suspected was the reason he'd kissed him.

He couldn't imagine Tyler, being as young as he was, would want him of all people. He'd just hit forty, and he had three kids, two of them adults who had to be around the same age as Tyler. He was tired, and even though his family was safe now, he was still terrified that something would happen to them. He remembered the months after he lost his job all too well and never wanted to go through something like that again.

He never would. He and his family were safe with the Rosewood pack. This was their home now, and from what Matt had seen, the pack stood up for its members. They supported everyone, be it with help or money, and knowing that had lifted a heavy weight from his shoulders. He didn't have a job yet, but he'd get one soon, and in the meantime, he'd always be able to put food on the table thanks to the pack.

And that was all that mattered.

He parked in front of the house and looked up at it. It was nothing special, but to him, it was everything. Even before losing his job, he'd only been able to afford apartments. It had been a tight fit when the boys still lived with them, but like everything else, they'd made it work. He was glad they didn't have to anymore. Doyle didn't live with them, and it wouldn't be long before Del left the house. It was probably too big for just Matt and Cora, but it gave her space to move around and play.

But right now, Matt didn't want to think about Cora. She was safe and having fun, and her being with a friend gave Matt the opportunity to finally ask Tyler what was going on between them.

Part of him thought there was nothing there and that he'd imagined everything. He should believe that, because there was no way someone like Tyler should be with him. It wasn't just an age thing or the fact that Matt already had three kids. It was also that Tyler was just starting to live, while Matt was tired and ready to settle down. Tyler might want to go back home, or if he didn't have a home, to explore the world and get to know people. Maybe he'd want to move to a city and have fun.

Matt, on the other hand, was perfectly happy in a small town. He'd skipped the part of his life where he'd been supposed to go out every night, meet people, and get drunk. He'd already had kids when his friends did that, and that had been fine with him. He wasn't going to start going to bars at forty years old, both because he was too old for that and because by the time it was nine PM, he was usually sleepy.

But he didn't want to hold Tyler back. Tyler needed to do whatever he wanted to do, and Matt had no idea what that was. He wouldn't find out without asking, so he got out of the car and headed inside the house.

Tyler had been nowhere to be seen when Matt and Cora

had left. Now, though, Matt could hear sounds coming from the kitchen, so that was where he went.

Tyler was singing. His voice was nice, soft, and gentle, and it was clear he hadn't heard that Matt was back. When Matt found him, he was cleaning the stove, his back to the door. His head bopped with the rhythm of his song, and all the tension was gone from his body.

Matt hated that because of the kiss, Tyler had retreated into himself. He wanted Tyler to spread his wings, not to isolate himself over something as stupid as a kiss.

But they needed to talk about it and what it meant. If they didn't, Matt would obsess over it. He was half in love with Tyler already and needed to know where they stood. He might not think Tyler would want anything to do with him, but he couldn't help but hope. He wanted things to get better. If there was a chance at all, he wanted to be with Tyler. It was ridiculous, but he couldn't help how he felt. Besides, Tyler had been the one to kiss him. He might have just needed support and to be close to someone, and if that was the case, Matt would give him that.

But he prayed there was something more growing between them.

Before he could say anything, there was a knock on the front door. He quickly retreated into the hallway, not wanting whoever it was to bother Tyler. If Tyler was alone in the house, he never answered the door. He was too skittish, and Matt would never ask him to go against his feelings just to see who it was. If he heard the knock, he'd either stay in the kitchen or go back upstairs to his room to avoid seeing whoever it was.

Sometimes, Matt wished he could do the same. He didn't want to talk to whoever was there, but he still went to open it in case it had something to do with Tyler or Pembroke. Angus was still looking for Ryland's brother, and eventually, he'd find him. Matt doubted he'd be involved in the rescue, but Tyler would want to know that his friend had been found.

Matt swung open the door, expecting a pack member or someone from the rescue group. The sight that greeted him on the porch was enough to make him freeze. He stared at the woman, his brain unable to comprehend what he was seeing.

He hadn't seen Pamela in six years. When she'd brought Cora to him, she's just given birth, and it had shown. She'd been a little frumpy, and he'd been angry at her, so he hadn't taken the time to ask her how she was or if she needed anything. She'd made what she needed obvious. She didn't want Cora, and she wanted Matt to raise her. Matt had taken the baby, and Pamela had left. The adoption had been complicated because of that, but eventually, it had gone through, and Matt had believed he'd never see Pamela again.

Pamela looked so different she might as well be another woman. She wore a tight black dress and red lipstick, and her hair was neatly arranged around her face. She had heels on that made her almost as tall as Matt, and she was holding a sleek and expensive-looking handbag. They were the same age, but Matt felt so much older next to her.

It wasn't that he didn't take care of himself. He was still recovering from losing his job, being terrified that he and his children would be homeless, then finding the pack and becoming a member, and he'd never cared much about his appearance.

Pamela smiled. "Matt."

"What are you doing here?" Matt asked. His voice came out slightly trembling, and he hated that. He didn't want to show Pamela how scared he was of her presence here. Clearly, this time she wasn't here to give him another one of her kids.

That meant she was here for Cora.

Doyle and Del were adults, so Pamela could do nothing to

them. She couldn't take them away or force them to have a relationship with her. Cora was different because she was only six, and Matt was really panicking at the thought of Pamela taking her away from him.

She was still smiling. "You're not inviting me in?"

Matt didn't want to, but it would be better than doing this on the porch.

He cleared his throat and stepped aside. "We can go to the living room. You can stay until you've talked to me, but not one second longer." He wasn't taking her to the kitchen, mostly because he needed to retreat there for a few seconds and gather himself, but also because he was afraid Tyler was still there. Whatever Pamela was here for, Matt would have a fight on his hands, and he needed to shake off the shock and terror.

Even if Pamela was here to take Cora, Matt wouldn't allow her to do so. He was ready to fight, and for the first time ever, he wouldn't be fighting alone.

Tyler had heard the front door, so he knew Matt was back and that there was someone with him. He had no idea who it was, but he'd heard a woman's voice, and he'd decided it was better to stay as far away from her and Matt as he could. He didn't want to know who she was and why she was here. He didn't want to meet her and have to introduce himself.

He swallowed and focused on cleaning the stove, even though it was already clean. Matt had said he didn't have anyone in his life, but clearly, he was into women since he had kids. Had he decided to date a woman? Was she someone from the pack?

He'd told Tyler he was taking Cora to a friend's house, yet he'd come back with a woman. What was happening? And what was Tyler supposed to do? Had Matt forgotten that he was there? The thought of him bringing home a woman to spend time with her made Tyler want to throw up, even though he didn't have a say in what Matt did and with whom.

He wasn't surprised to hear Matt come into the kitchen. He steeled himself, ready to face whatever was about to happen, and turned.

Matt was terrified.

His eyes were wide and he was pale, and when he gripped the back of one of the chairs, Tyler could see his hands were trembling. Matt's reaction didn't make sense, but clearly, something was wrong.

"What is it?" Tyler asked, rushing to his side. He'd been avoiding Matt for the past few days, but that was over now because Matt needed him.

Matt swallowed and pressed closer to Tyler when Tyler put a hand against his back. "It's my ex."

The bottom of Tyler's stomach dropped. "Cora's mother?"

Matt nodded. "She's also Doyle and Del's mother, but yes. She's here."

Tyler didn't know the story, but he wished he did. He wanted to know why seeing her scared Matt so much. It probably had to do with Cora, and Tyler wondered if the woman was here to take her daughter back.

He hadn't understood when Matt had explained that his ex had left Cora with him without hesitation. Matt hadn't gone into details, but Tyler had been curious to know why she wasn't in Cora's life. Matt had never even mentioned her by name, which, as far as Tyler was concerned, was a sign that he didn't care about her. If anything, when he talked about her, he sounded angry, which made sense considering the woman had abandoned her kids with Matt and left.

There were many pieces Tyler was missing from the story, and now wasn't the moment to ask. Now, the only thing he could do was be there for Matt. "What do you need me to do?"

"I don't know." Matt shook his head. "You should go upstairs or leave the house. I don't know why she's here, but I think it would be better if she didn't see you. I don't want her to know about anyone in my life."

Tyler wasn't surprised, and to be honest, he was even glad. He didn't want to see this woman. He couldn't help but wonder if she was here to take both Cora *and* Matt back. Matt was afraid, but he didn't know what she wanted yet. What if she explained that she wanted back into Matt and Cora's lives? What if she said she regretted leaving them and that she wanted another chance?

Matt would probably agree to have her spend time with Cora, if anything because he'd feel he owed it to Cora. She'd never known her mother, and as far as Tyler was concerned, now wasn't the time for her to start, but it was none of his business. He needed to stay out of it, even though he wanted nothing more than to stand by Matt's side and face this woman, whoever she was.

But instead, he nodded. "I'll go upstairs."

"Good. Stay there until I come to you, all right?" He didn't wait for Tyler's answer. He turned, squared his shoulders, and after taking a deep breath, went back to the living room.

Tyler followed him.

He'd said he'd go upstairs, and he would, but he wanted to find out what was going on first. He needed to know and wouldn't if he didn't listen. He felt bad about lying to Matt and spying on him, but he wanted to be there if Matt needed him.

He didn't think Matt and his ex-wife would end up fighting, at least not physically. Matt would never hurt anyone, let alone a woman and the mother of his children. But, just in case, Tyler wanted to be close by. His gargoyle was ready to jump into whatever was happening if they needed to protect him, and Tyler agreed.

He hovered by the living room door, making sure no one inside could see him. For now, everything was quiet, and he pressed his back against the wall, holding his breath.

"You look good," Matt said.

"Thank you. You don't look too bad, either."

Tyler sucked in a breath. He thought he recognized the voice, but it wasn't possible. It couldn't be Pamela, the woman who'd organized the auctions and who'd made his life hell for so long.

Right?

Matt hadn't mentioned his ex-wife by name or what she did with her life. Tyler tried to remember every detail, but Matt had only said a few things, and they weren't enough to identify her, especially since they were old news.

That wasn't enough for Tyler to know for sure if she was the woman who'd hurt him so badly.

"I have to say it's a surprise to see you here. I didn't expect to see you again after you left Cora with me," Matt said.

"I'm sorry about that. I shouldn't have dumped her on you and vanished, but it was the only thing I could do at the time. I knew you'd do right by her."

"Why are you here? Is it because of Cora? Because I'm telling you right now, if you think you can take her back, I'm not letting you. She's my daughter. I'm the one who raised her and was there for her for the past six years."

There was a moment of silence. Tyler almost expected the woman to say she was here to take Cora, and he wasn't sure how his gargoyle would react. It was protective of Cora and Matt, and it saw them as their family. Tyler did, too. He had half a mind to step into the room and tell Matt's ex-wife that she wasn't taking Cora, but he needed to stay out of it. It was none of his business, and Matt had asked him to stay away. Tyler didn't know how he'd react if he found himself in front of Pamela.

"I realize you're the only parent she's known since birth. I just want to reconnect with her. She's six, and while I'm sure she'll be confused, she's young enough to need her mother," Matt's ex said.

"She doesn't need her mother. She never has, and the fact that you've now decided you want to be her mother doesn't have anything to do with her. I won't let you hurt her."

"I'm not here to hurt her. I'm here to get to know her and reconnect with the boys if I can. Are they here? I want to talk to them. And where is Cora?"

Matt's voice was steely when he answered. "I'm alone in the house. The boys, as you call them, are adults and have partners. Cora is at a friend's house and will stay there until you leave."

"She's my daughter."

"You didn't seem to think she was when you left her with me."

"I didn't have a choice. I know you adopted Cora, but I'm her mother. Any judge would know it's important for her to have a relationship with me."

The silence was heavy with tension. Tyler didn't understand what was happening, but he didn't have to in order to know that Matt was terrified. That was enough to make him angry, but he resisted the urge to barge in. He didn't want to ruin everything, whatever that everything was. He was also scared.

"So you *are* here to take Cora back," Matt said.

"I already told you why I'm here. I want to get to know my daughter. I want to reconnect with my sons. For now, that's all."

Tyler didn't have to be there to know what she wasn't saying. *It was all she wanted for now*, but if Matt didn't give it to her, she wouldn't hesitate to take more.

Matt was freaking out, but he tried not to show it. He didn't want Pamela to know that she was winning.

Because she wasn't. Matt was Cora's father, and that was that.

The problem was that from the way Pamela looked, it was clear she'd somehow come into money. Knowing her, knowing how she behaved when she wanted something, Matt was sure that she wouldn't hesitate to hire the best lawyer she could find. She wouldn't care that it would be better for Cora to stay with Matt. She'd just care that Matt had something that she wanted, even if she only wanted it for a moment. Matt was sure that after she realized how much work Cora was, Pamela would dump her again. In the meantime, though, she could create a lot of pain for everyone, and Matt didn't want that to happen.

But he didn't know what to do. He wanted to call Doyle and Del and have them support him, but he also didn't want them to be hurt by the fact that their mother was back. Tyler was out of the question, so who did that leave?

The sound of a car parking in front of the house almost made Matt smile. Whoever it was, he was ready to kiss them for interrupting the conversation.

"Let me see who it is," he told Pamela.

He rushed out of the living room. There was some movement in the hallway, but he ignored it. He was already taking out his phone. He texted the mother of the friend Cora was staying with to ask her if Cora could stay for the rest of the day, mentioning he had an emergency. By the time he pulled the door open, he had confirmation, which was a relief. He also texted Cam, just in case. He was Matt's alpha, so he needed to know something was going on.

Seeing Del and Angus was both a relief and made Matt feel

awful. He didn't want to involve his son, but he needed support. His thoughts went to Tyler, but he knew he couldn't bring him into this. Tyler was healing and finding out what he wanted in life. He didn't need to be involved in whatever Pamela was planning. Del would be whether Matt wanted it or not because he was Pamela's son, but Tyler needed to stay away.

Matt stepped on the porch and quickly closed the door behind himself. Angus and Del both stared at him. Clearly, he didn't have to say anything for them to know that something had happened.

Matt raked a hand through his hair, wondering how to bring up Pamela. He didn't have much time, which meant it was better to put everything out there.

"Dad?" Del asked.

"I need you to stay calm."

Unfortunately, Del was the one with the most volatile temper. Doyle would have freaked out, but he'd have been quiet about it. On the other hand, Del wouldn't hesitate to yell at his mother. Matt was pretty sure that would be the worst thing any of them could do, but he wasn't sure Del would be able to see that.

"I don't know if I can promise that. I don't know what's happening."

Matt hated doing this. "Your mother is here." Del stared at him. Clearly, he didn't know what to make of it, which made two of them. "I need you to give her a chance and to listen to her," Matt continued.

Del's expression turned hard. He was pissed, but Matt needed him to stop and think about the situation.

"Why would I do that?" Del asked in a lethal tone that didn't bode well for Pamela.

"Because she's also Cora's mother, and Cora is only six years old. I can't risk losing her. I can't risk for your mother to get custody of Cora."

Del stared. It was as if he didn't understand what Matt was saying, but then, *Matt* didn't understand what was happening. Everything had been so normal this morning. He'd been planning on talking to Tyler and, if he was lucky, kissing him again. Now, everything was a mess, and Matt didn't know what to do.

"Has she said anything?" Del asked.

It dawned on Matt that Del was afraid to lose Cora, too. He wouldn't want that to happen, which was what Matt had hoped for. If that made Del listen to him and give Pamela a chance, he needed to tell him everything. "She wants to talk to you and Doyle. She, well, she said she wants to fix her relationship with the two of you and Cora."

"Why? She never cared."

What Pamela had done had hurt Doyle and Del. When Pamela had left, they'd been old enough to understand that she wasn't coming back. They'd gotten to know her as their mother, and they'd been hurt. Matt still remembered how they'd cried for her to come back, but the only time she had was to bring Cora to them. Del had been fourteen, and he'd been pissed. Matt didn't want a repeat of the screaming that had happened back then.

He rubbed his face, trying to find the right words. "I don't know why she's here." Matt had a hard time believing that she really wanted to reconnect with her children. "I don't know if she's telling the truth or if she's lying. Either way, it would be easy for her to get Cora. I'm not her father, which means I don't have the same rights as her."

"But you raised her."

"I did, and I adopted her. It doesn't mean your mother wouldn't manage to get her if she tried, though." Especially if she had more money than Matt. If she could afford the best lawyers, he would have no chance.

Del's body language showed obvious anger, so Matt was surprised when he said, "Fine. I'll talk to her."

He turned toward the door, and Matt expected the worst, like him yelling at Pamela as soon as he saw her. He was about to intervene, but Angus did, as was right since he was Del's mate. "You should probably look less like you're about to take her on in a fight," Angus said as he pressed a hand to Del's back.

"You don't know what she did to us," Del spat out.

"Not the details, but I know enough. If she's here to fix her relationship with you, you can't look angry when you meet her."

"I don't care what she wants. I just need her to leave us alone."

Matt had to agree with his son there. He wanted Pamela to leave them alone and never come back. Was it too much to ask? Maybe she was here because the universe thought that things were going too well in Matt's life recently.

"Unfortunately, it might not be an option. Let's just see what's going on, all right?"

They went inside, Del stomping all the way there. In the entrance, he looked around as if looking for something, and Matt realized what that something was. "Cora is at a play date," he whispered. "And I asked Tyler to stay in his room." He was glad he'd thought to do so. He had no doubt Pamela would use Tyler's presence in the house against him.

"That's good to know. Are the other child's parents aware they shouldn't bring Cora home?"

Del's question almost made Matt smile. Del might have been fourteen when Cora appeared in his life, but he'd always loved and fiercely protected her. If something were to happen to Matt, he knew Doyle and Del would make sure Cora was all right. "I texted them and Cam to let them know what was going on."

Del didn't hesitate now that he knew his sister wasn't around. He walked into the living room with his shoulders square and a resolute expression. Matt didn't know how he did it. He was terrified and quaking in his shoes.

Pamela was sitting on the couch, looking at her phone. She looked up when she heard Del and stared without reacting to him. Matt wondered if she even recognized her son. The last time she'd seen him, he'd been a teenager, but he wasn't anymore, even though he was only twenty. He was a man with a life and a mate, and Matt couldn't be more proud. He was also proud of the fact that Del didn't immediately start yelling.

But Pamela put her phone in her bag and got to her feet. "Del?" she asked.

Del stared. He didn't react in any way. He just stared at her as if she was something on the bottom of his shoe. He might not be yelling, but his hatred was obvious for everyone to see.

"You've grown so much since the last time I saw you. You had to be ten or eleven," Pamela continued, but her smile was slipping.

"Fourteen. It's when you brought Cora home."

"I'm sorry."

"What are you sorry for?" Del asked.

Maybe he'd be able to get an actual answer out of his mother. Matt didn't believe she was here just to reconnect with her kids, but he prayed he was wrong.

Pamela looked sad. "Everything. I was never a mother to you and your siblings, and I realize now how wrong it was."

"Is that why you're here? To be a mother?"

"If you'll let me. I want to atone for what I did to you. None of it was right, and I hope that eventually you'll forgive me, but I won't push for you to. I only ask for a chance to make you see that I've changed."

If Matt believed her, maybe he'd say yes to all of this. The problem was that he was convinced she had another reason to be here, and it couldn't be good.

Tyler went upstairs when Del and Angus came in with Matt, but he didn't go far. He listened to Del talk to his mother, and he wasn't surprised to hear that Del wasn't happy with her presence. He didn't sound scared like Matt had been, but rather angry.

Tyler had no idea what was going on, and he wanted answers. He needed them so he could protect his mate and their family. He hadn't been here long and didn't know what Del and Doyle would think of him being Matt's mate. Hell, he didn't even know what *Matt* would think of it.

But he didn't care. Even if no one wanted him here after they found out, he could make sure they were okay from afar, especially if Matt's ex was the woman involved with the auction.

Tyler told himself there was no way she could be, but her voice was too similar.

Was it a coincidence? Or did this mean that Matt and the pack were somehow involved in the auctions? Tyler couldn't breathe when he thought of that possibility, but he forced himself to be rational. There was no way Cam or Matt were involved with the auctions. Pamela, if she was Matt's ex-wife, hadn't been in his life for the past six years.

Tyler tried to remember when she'd started being involved in the auctions. Initially, it had only been Fulton and an array of assistants, but about four years ago, when Tyler had been sold back to them because his owner didn't like him anymore, she'd suddenly been there. She and Fulton were involved, and she'd never mentioned having an ex-husband or children. Of course, she wouldn't have told Tyler about it, but she'd never struck him as someone who wanted a family. She was too cold and evil.

The sounds of footsteps brought Tyler's attention back to the moment. He could hear heels striking the floor, so he knew someone was taking Matt's ex to the front door.

"I'll be back," she said.

"I really wish you wouldn't."

"These are my children, Matt, and if I want them, I'll take them. I always get what I want."

Her voice made Tyler shiver. He wanted to know if Matt's ex and Pamela were the same person, but at the same time, he was terrified, so he stayed where he was until he heard the door close, then a car door opening and closing. He crept down the stairs in time to hear Matt and Del.

"We'll do everything we can to keep Cora with us," Del promised.

"I know." Matt's voice was muffled, but Tyler could hear the pain in his tone.

"I don't know why she's here, but we'll find out and make sure she can't hurt us."

Matt and Del needed to talk, so instead of going to Matt like he wanted, Tyler headed to the kitchen. He stayed there while the three had a conversation, but as soon as the front door opened and closed again, he went to find Matt.

He wasn't surprised to see he was still in the living room, sitting on the couch, looking like his life was crumbling around him.

Matt looked up when he heard Tyler and got to his feet. "I thought I told you to stay in your room until I came to get you."

Tyler crossed his arms over his chest. He understood why Matt thought he needed protection, but he wasn't as weak as everyone believed. He'd be dead if he were. "What happened? What did she want?"

Matt rubbed his face. He looked like he could use a nap, but Tyler doubted he'd be able to sleep. "To talk to Doyle and

Del. To reconnect with them and get to know Cora."

"What did you tell her?" Tyler didn't ask if her name was Pamela. He was too scared to find out that it was. He'd have to face that reality eventually, but for now, he needed to know that he and Matt were a team.

The problem was that he didn't know what they were. The only thing they'd shared was a kiss, and Tyler hadn't been honest with Matt. He needed to be, but he didn't know if now was the best moment. Matt might be happy to find out they were mates and that he wouldn't have to face this alone, but he might also get angry, which wasn't what Tyler wanted.

"I told her to leave, and she did. She won't stop until she gets Cora, though. I don't understand what she wants from my daughter, but I'm scared." Matt sighed. "But you don't have to worry about that."

"Don't say that." Tyler's voice was harder than he'd intended, but maybe it was good for Matt to know he was angry.

Matt seemed surprised. "You have much better things to focus on. You need to heal and deal with your new life, and you don't need my complications."

Tyler was getting angrier with every word that came out of Matt's mouth. He realized it was his fault for not being honest with Matt, but his family was being threatened, and he wouldn't stand for that. "I'm not fragile," he snapped.

Matt's eyes widened. "I never said you were. But you've been through a lot, and you're so young."

"I'm not that young. How old do you think I am?" Because that seemed to be a source of confusion, and it was easily dealt with.

Matt hesitated. "Around Del and Doyle's age. Del is twenty, and Doyle is twenty-two."

Tyler shook his head. "I know I look young, but I'm not." His curly blond hair, blue eyes, and the fact that he was so short were a curse. People didn't take him seriously and didn't believe he could defend himself or stand up for himself. Matt felt the same, but Tyler would show him how wrong he was.

"Even if you're older than Doyle, you can't be more than twenty-five," Matt argued.

"I'm twenty-nine, almost thirty. And I might not have been allowed to live my life, but that's over now, and I'm ready to take on the future."

"But what's happening with my family and me isn't your problem."

"How can it not be my problem when you're my mate?"

Tyler hadn't meant to tell Matt like that, but it was as if he couldn't get through. Matt wanted to protect him and shield him from whatever was going on, and maybe he wasn't wrong to want that. No matter what he'd said, Tyler did feel slightly fragile.

But that wouldn't stop him from fighting.

He moved closer, ignoring the way Matt was staring at him. Matt probably had many questions, but Tyler needed to ask something first. He needed to know.

"Do you want her?"

Matt frowned. "Please tell me you're not talking about my ex-wife."

"I am. If you want to get back with her, I won't like it, but I'll step back, even though you're my mate."

"I never wanted to get back with her after she left the boys and me. That hasn't changed, even though it's been years. If anything, I hate her even more than I did back then." He hesitated. "Is it true? I'm your mate?"

Tyler sighed. "It is. I shouldn't have told you like this, but I need you to stop seeing me as someone you have to protect. I can protect myself and you and your family. You've seen my gargoyle form." He sucked in a breath. Since he and Matt were talking, he might as well be completely honest. "I realize we only recently met and that I'm a mess. There's nothing I can do about that or my past. But I need you to allow me to protect you and the rest of your family. Both my gargoyle and I see you as ours, and I'm sure we can help. I don't know what your ex-wife wants, if she actually wants a relationship with her children or if there's something more to it, but as long as you want me in your life, I think we should face the situation together."

"I'm your mate," Matt repeated.

Tyler smiled. "You are, and I will love and cherish you for the rest of our lives. I'll be by your side when you face your ex-wife and whatever she throws at you. I'm not going anywhere, Matt. As long as you say yes, it's you and me against the world from now on." That was all Tyler had ever wanted and dreamed of, all he'd been afraid to hope for when he'd been in that cage.

So when Matt nodded and stepped forward to pull him into his arms, Tyler's heart exploded, or at least, it felt like it did. Whatever happened next, they'd face it together and be stronger for it. Tyler was convinced of that as he curled into Matt's arms, allowing Matt to comfort him and, at the same time, comforting Matt.

CHAPTER FIVE

Matt bounced his knee. He needed to get rid of the tension, and this was the only way he could do it while sitting in the waiting room. He was pretty sure he was annoying the few other people there, but he ignored them and focused on himself.

He hadn't been able to stop thinking about Pamela and what she'd said since she'd come over to the house yesterday. He'd barely slept, and the only reason he wasn't freaking out was that Tyler was sitting next to him.

They were here thanks to Cam. After Pamela had left and Matt and Tyler had talked, Matt's phone had blown up. First, it had been Doyle, freaking out about his mother being back. He had more memories of her when he was a child since he was two years older than Del, and he'd always been softer than his brother. He didn't know if he wanted a relationship with his mother, but he wasn't dismissing her right out like Del. He was willing to give her a chance.

If Matt was honest with himself, he was on Del's side when it came to this. He didn't want anything to do with Pamela. He didn't want her to be in his life, and he wanted her nowhere near Cora. He hadn't told Cora about Pamela yet and had no intention of doing so.

Which was why he was here, waiting to talk to a lawyer.

Apparently, the man was Cam's friend. It was the only reason he'd agreed to see them so quickly, and Matt understood how lucky he was. Now that he didn't have a job, it would have been hard for him to find the money to pay a lawyer, and it needed to be a good one. Pamela looked like she could afford to bury Matt under legal stuff and snatch Cora while he wasn't looking. He'd been extremely careful after Cora had come home last night, checking the locks obsessively, to the point where she'd noticed. He didn't want to worry her, but he was freaking out, and he thought she'd picked up on that.

A soft hand landed on his knee and squeezed. He stopped bouncing and looked at Tyler, opening his mouth to apologize.

Tyler shook his head. "Don't. It's normal to be nervous and to find an outlet. It's just kind of annoying."

Matt looked away. Tyler shouldn't be here. Even after the conversation they'd had yesterday, even after Matt had found out he was Tyler's mate, it didn't feel right to involve him.

Matt was used to keeping his problems to himself. Most of his life, he hadn't had anyone to share them with, especially after Pamela had left and he'd found himself alone with two children, then three. He hadn't been about to share his struggle with them, so he'd never talked much about them. Doyle and Del had been old enough to realize when Matt had lost his job, but Matt hadn't wanted to burden them with that. It had almost ended in a disaster, which had reinforced the feeling that it was best to keep them out of his problems. He was used to shouldering everything on his own, but clearly, that was about to change if it hadn't already.

When he thought about last night, he could only focus on how fierce Tyler had been. He'd been right when he said that Matt had been dismissive of him, but thankfully, he understood that Matt had only done it because he cared. He hadn't known Tyler was his mate, and he hadn't thought it was right for him to involve him in a situation it would be better for him to stay out of. Pamela had never been a bad person, but she was selfish, and Matt knew she'd use anything she could to get what she wanted. He didn't understand why it was Cora, but Pamela wouldn't hesitate to use whatever she could against him, including the fact that he didn't have a job and Tyler.

But Tyler was there, and Matt didn't want to push him away. More than ever, he needed a partner to support him, and while he felt guilty about dumping all of that on Tyler, for now, Tyler was dealing with it admirably. He'd pushed Matt until he explained more about the situation with Pamela, and once he'd been satisfied with the answers Matt had given him, he'd nodded and kissed him.

That was when Doyle had burst into the house because Del had told him about Pamela, so nothing more had happened because Matt had spent the next half hour calming his son down. It was just as well. Matt had been overwhelmed, and he wanted to take his time when it came to his mate.

His mate. As a human, Matt had never thought he'd have a mate. He'd watched it happen first to Doyle, then to Del, and he'd been happy for his sons, but he hadn't truly believed it would happen to him, too. In a way, he probably should have since he now lived with the pack, but he'd been focused on Cora and their new life, which had been fine for him.

But it wasn't just Matt and Cora anymore. It was Matt and Cora and Tyler, and it would take some time to get used to. Tyler had taken to it as if he'd always been in their lives. From day one, he'd attempted to take care of them, even when Matt had tried to convince him not to. He and Cora liked each other, and now, he was here, ready to support Matt. Matt wasn't sure what he'd do if it weren't for Tyler, and he didn't want to find out.

He didn't want to face this alone.

The office door opened, and a woman came out. She'd been at the desk earlier when Matt and Tyler had arrived, and since she'd told them to wait there, she was probably the lawyer's assistant. She'd been in the office for a good five minutes now, but thankfully, she nodded at them.

"You can go in. Mr. Hewitt is waiting for you."

Matt got to his feet, Tyler following suit. To Matt's surprise, Tyler took his hand and squeezed. Maybe Matt shouldn't be surprised. Tyler had kept to himself when he'd first moved in with Matt and his family, but since last night, he'd been much freer with gestures of affection. Matt hadn't realized it before, but it was clear that Tyler had held back because he hadn't wanted to freak Matt out. Now, he didn't have to anymore. Matt knew they were mates and was more than okay with it. Tyler seemed to have taken that as a go-ahead regarding PDA.

He clung to Tyler's hand as they walked into the office.

Matt wasn't sure what he'd expected from the lawyer. He didn't even know if the man was a shifter, but he wasn't sure it mattered either way. Matt and Cora were human, as was Pamela, so this would be dealt with by the courts if things went that far, not by the pack.

"Welcome, and sorry for the wait," the man behind the desk said as he gestured toward the chairs on the other side of his desk.

Matt and Tyler sat. Tyler didn't let go of Matt's hand, for which Matt was grateful. He felt like he might be about to fly apart and needed Tyler to keep him together.

Preston Hewitt was a good-looking man. His blond hair was neatly combed, and his brown eyes sparkled with interest as Matt and Tyler settled in front of him. He leaned forward, and his open expression made Matt feel welcome. He didn't think he'd ever felt that way when dealing with lawyers.

"When Cam called me yesterday, I was surprised to hear from him. He's not one who usually needs my help for anything, especially when it comes to humans," Hewitt said.

"He's my alpha and insisted on me coming here," Matt explained.

Hewitt nodded. "I see. I was surprised to find out he had humans in his pack, but maybe I shouldn't be. He's always been a welcoming guy, and from what I've seen over the past several years, he's made a habit of collecting strays."

Matt wouldn't call himself a stray, but he understood what the lawyer was saying. "Thank you for seeing us, Mr. Hewitt. I'm Matt, and this is Tyler."

"Call me Preston. I'm a friend of Cam's, and if you're one of his pack members, it makes us at least friendly. Now, why don't you tell me what's going on? Cam didn't give me many details, and I'm curious."

Matt swallowed. He liked that Preston was a no-nonsense kind of guy and that he'd gone straight to the point. Having to explain what was happening made Matt's stomach churn, but this was what he was here for. Hopefully, it was the last time he needed to tell his story to anyone.

And the last time he had to deal with Pamela.

Tyler didn't know what to think of the lawyer, but he didn't see another way to deal with this problem. He couldn't do anything, but Matt needed help, and this was the only way he would get it. Human laws were confusing, and Tyler doubted he'd understand much if he tried to make sense of it, but that was why they were here—so that Preston could do that for them.

Tyler didn't know the entire story yet. Matt had explained how his ex-wife had left when Del and Doyle were young, had come back to give Cora to him, then left again, but that was all Tyler knew. He'd wanted to find out more, but he was also terrified. He was sure that Pamela was Matt's ex-wife, and he'd need to say something about that, but he couldn't seem to be able to. For now, anyway, he needed to focus on Matt and Cora. Whatever Pamela was up to could be dealt with later, or at least, Tyler hoped so.

"To make a long story short, I married my high school girl-friend when she got pregnant. We had two sons before she left and we divorced. She didn't see them for ten years. When she came back, she had a daughter." Matt hesitated. "I'm not her biological father, but I raised her anyway. I adopted Cora."

The lawyer was taking notes and nodding as Matt spoke. He looked up, an understanding expression on his face. "So you took care of the little girl even though she isn't your daughter."

"She *is* my daughter," Matt said, his voice going hard.

"You're right. I meant your biological daughter."

"I couldn't let my ex-wife leave her who knows where. Cora was just a baby back then, and my sons' sister. It didn't matter to me that we weren't related by blood. I raised her for the past six years."

"But since you're here, I take it there's a problem with your ex-wife."

Matt's jaw tightened, and Tyler squeezed his hand. He didn't miss the way the lawyer's gaze flickered to their linked fingers, but he kept his focus on Matt. He had no doubt Preston would ask about their relationship once Matt was done talking, and Tyler wasn't sure how they'd answer.

That was a problem for later.

"Yesterday, there was a knock on my door, and it was her. She hasn't seen Cora since she was a newborn and her sons since they were fourteen and sixteen. Now, she suddenly wants a relationship with all three of them. She kept saying that Cora needs her mother, that she wants to reconnect with her sons." Matt leaned forward. "I'm not worried about Del and Doyle. They're adults, and if they want a relationship with their mother, I won't try to stop them. But some of the things she said yesterday worry me. She didn't outright threaten me, but she implied that she wouldn't hesitate to pull lawyers into the situation if I didn't give her what she wants."

Preston tapped his pen on the pad he'd been using to take notes. "So she hasn't been in your life for the past six years?"

"I'd say she hasn't been in my life for the past decade. She reappeared briefly to leave her daughter with me, but I wouldn't count that as being in my life."

Preston nodded and took another note. "And you adopted your daughter?"

"Yes. I already emailed you all the paperwork. The adoption is official, so Cora is my daughter."

"Did her mother give up her parental rights?"

"She did."

Tyler wanted to ask questions, but it was better for him to stay out of it. This was Matt's story, and Tyler felt Preston was a good lawyer. Cam wouldn't have told them to come here today if he weren't, and Preston was clearly interested in their case.

Tyler didn't know when it had happened, but he trusted the alpha. Maybe it was because Cam had welcomed him with open arms even when he didn't know him, or maybe it was because Matt trusted him. Whatever the reason, it didn't matter. The only thing that did was that they were here, and hopefully, Preston would be able to keep Matt's ex-wife away.

Tyler was ready to do pretty much anything for that to happen. Matt and Cora were his family, and he wasn't letting them go. He also wouldn't allow anyone to hurt them.

He must have made a sound, because Preston's gaze jumped to him. They stared at each other for a moment, and when Preston spoke again, his focus was on Tyler. "What about you? Are you Matt's partner?"

Tyler and Matt looked at each other. Tyler didn't know if Matt being his mate would help with Cora or make things more complicated, but he needed to be honest with Preston. The lawyer was on their side, and he'd tell them whether or not to mention this.

"Matt is my mate," Tyler explained. "I'm a gargoyle shifter."

Preston's eyes widened. "I don't think I've ever met a gargoyle shifter."

"Well, you have now. Matt and I only recently met, but he and Cora are my family."

Preston nodded. "Of course."

"I don't know if the fact that we haven't been together long will be a problem, but I'm not leaving Matt. We'll both fight for our family."

Preston leaned back in his chair and linked his fingers together. He stared at Tyler for a moment before nodding. "I don't want to make any promises, because things happen and go to shit, but from what I see, I don't think that Matt's ex-wife has any way to get Cora. Not only did she abandon her sons, but she also abandoned her daughter and didn't show any interest in her for the past six years. Clearly, she was right to leave Cora in Matt's hands because he's a loving father, but since she gave up her parental rights and Matt legally adopted Cora, she doesn't have a leg to stand on. That doesn't mean she can't create trouble, though."

"What kind of trouble?" Matt asked.

"Of the legal kind. Depending on how wealthy she is, she could afford to hire lawyers who'll pull you around and make you despair. From what you're telling me, she's used to you going along with whatever she wants."

"You mean like taking Cora in? It's the best thing I ever did."

Preston raised a hand. "I didn't say it wasn't. I admire you, Matt. Not many men would have taken in a baby they knew for sure wasn't theirs, and considering the history with your ex-wife, I'm impressed. I don't think she can get Cora or even visitation, but she could make your life difficult." Preston's gaze flickered to Tyler. "She might even manage to get a judge to listen to her, but between the fact that you've adopted Cora, that you raised her as your own, and that you can provide her with a stable family, I don't see how anyone in their right mind could give your ex-wife visitation."

"There's something else," Tyler quickly said. He didn't want to talk about what he'd gone through, but it might come up eventually, especially if Matt's ex-wife was Pamela.

He really needed to tell someone about all of this.

"I'm listening," Preston said.

"My life hasn't been easy. My parents kicked me out when I was fifteen and I came out to them. I lived on the streets for a few years before I was taken in by someone I thought wanted to help me. Instead, they sold me."

Preston grimaced. "Cam mentioned something about an auction house and people buying and selling shifters. I'm sorry you had to go through that."

"I just want to make sure it won't be a problem when it comes to this."

"I don't see why it should. You'll need time to heal from your experience, but from what I see, it doesn't stop you from being an integral part of Matt's life, which means you're part of Cora's life, too. She has two parents thanks to the bond between you and Matt, and she's only known Matt as a parent and now you. I'm sure she's a healthy and happy little girl and that Matt has done everything he could to take care of her to the best of his ability. You live with a healthy and wealthy pack, which means you have protection and people to support you through anything life might throw at you. All in all, I'm optimistic."

Tyler was happy to hear that. He expected that the fact that Pamela might be one of the people auctioning shifters didn't matter. From what Tyler had seen of her, she and her boyfriend were rich, so there would be no consequences for either of them. Tyler didn't even know if anyone involved in this would care that she was doing that. After all, Pamela was buying and selling shifters, not humans, and to some humans, that was all that mattered.

But Tyler couldn't keep this to himself indefinitely. The problem was that he knew it would freak Matt out even more. He didn't want Cora to go back to her mother, and he'd want it even less if he found out what kind of monster Pamela was.

The problem was that no one could promise Pamela wouldn't get her hands on Cora. If Matt knew what Pamela did, he'd be even more terrified, but Tyler didn't want to continue lying to him.

What was he supposed to do?

Matt could see there was something on Tyler's mind as they left the office. He didn't blame Tyler. After everything he'd gone through, he'd found his mate, only to end up in a familial fight over Cora. Matt might not have wanted to be involved if he had been in his place.

He almost snorted. Who was he trying to fool? If their roles had been reversed, he'd be in Tyler's place, supporting him. After all, like Tyler had said, they were a family. It might be because of the bond they shared, but it was as good a reason as any other, and if it meant they could keep Cora, Matt wouldn't hesitate to yell from the rooftops that he and Tyler were mates.

But something still worried Tyler, and Matt wanted to know what it was. The problem was that he felt he was using Tyler for this and didn't want to make it worse. Preston had almost been giddy when he'd been told about the bond because it meant that Cora had two parents, but it wasn't something Matt and Tyler had talked about. Tyler had been through incredible trauma, and becoming an instant father to a six-year-old might be too much for him, especially considering everything else.

"I'm sorry," Matt said once they reached the car.

Tyler frowned. "What are you sorry about?"

"Involving you in all of this." Matt dropped Tyler's hand and took a step back. "I'm sure this isn't what you imagined when you realized I was your mate."

"Well, it's not, but it's not your fault. You have nothing to do with the way your ex behaves or what she wants."

Matt rubbed his face. "I feel like I do. I feel like I should tell you to run as far and fast as you can and like I should protect you from all of this."

Tyler shook his head. "I don't need to be protected." He hesitated. "If anything, I feel that you and Cora need to be protected. You never told me your ex-wife's name."

Matt blinked, wondering where this had come from. "Does it matter?"

"I think it might."

Matt didn't understand, but he was ready to give Tyler anything he wanted. "Pamela."

Tyler briefly closed his eyes. His expression did something complicated that Matt couldn't read, and Matt sucked in a breath, wondering what had just happened. Why had Pamela's name created such a strong reaction in Tyler? What was happening?

"When I was in that place, there wasn't just Fulton, the guy who leads the auctions," Tyler explained. "There were the guards, of course, but Fulton doesn't work alone. His girlfriend helps him. She makes sure everyone has showered before an auction, gives us drugs if we're agitated, things like that. Fulton is only there before the auctions, and from what I know, he's the one who finds the people who buy and sell shifters to him. His girlfriend takes care of the merchandise."

"That's a horrible way to say it." But Matt knew it was something Tyler had probably heard time and time again when he'd been with those people.

"It is, but it's what we were to them."

"I'm sorry you had to go through all of that. I'm just not sure what it has to do with Pamela."

Tyler looked down.

It was almost as if he expected Matt to push him away, and Matt didn't understand why. He might have only found out that he was Tyler's mate yesterday, but he felt they'd become a team since the first time Tyler had stepped foot into the house. Hell, even before, when he'd been the only one Tyler had let close. He hadn't known why then, but he did now and couldn't have been happier.

Well, maybe if Pamela hadn't decided to fuck with his life again. He clung to the knowledge that he wasn't facing her alone this time around. Not only did he have Tyler, but there was also Cam and the pack, and Doyle and Del were adults. They'd support Matt through all of this.

"The woman, Fulton's girlfriend," Tyler said. "Her name was Pamela."

Matt had to think about that for a second. "And you think it's the same person? That's not possible." He didn't like Pamela and hated what she'd done to their kids, but she wasn't a bad person.

Was she?

Matt didn't know her. He felt like he never had, but over the past ten years, she'd no doubt changed, and from what he'd seen yesterday, it wasn't for the better. She'd always been selfish, as she'd shown when she left her children without a second thought. Clearly, she was doing well for herself, and she might be doing it by hurting shifters.

Matt leaned against the car, not caring one bit that it

needed to be washed. He rubbed his eyes, trying to make sense of all of this.

"I'm sorry," Tyler whispered. "I'm not sure it's her because I didn't see your ex-wife when she came to the house, but I heard her voice."

"And you recognized it." It was the only thing that made sense. Tyler wouldn't accuse anyone of hurting people if he weren't sure.

"I think I did, but I can't be sure until I see her. The name fits, though, and I think it would be too much of a coincidence if it weren't the same person. There's also the fact that she found you even though you recently moved."

Matt blinked and stared at Tyler. He hadn't thought about that, but now, he wondered how Pamela had managed that.

He'd moved a few times over the years, but Pamela had found him to give him Cora. Now, she'd found him again, and he wouldn't be worried normally, but he was suspicious because he hadn't just found a new apartment. He'd moved in with a pack he didn't know, and no one could have predicted that or would have thought to look for him there. How had Pamela known? There might be a simple explanation, but it might also be something more nefarious, especially if Tyler was right about the way she earned her money.

"I don't know what to make of any of this," Matt admitted.

"I don't think you have to make anything of it, at least for now. It's a lot to take in, especially with what I just told you. You need some time."

"I don't want you to have to deal with her if she's the person who hurt you."

"It doesn't matter. I'll be there for you and Cora, even if Pamela is the woman who hurt me. I want to be with you, Matt. I don't care if you use me and what happened to me to keep Cora. I'd do anything for you to be able to do that, and I will. I know you believe I have to heal, and maybe you're right. Having to heal doesn't mean I can't love and have a family, though. It doesn't mean I can't protect you."

Matt was in awe. He'd known Tyler was strong, but he was ready to face one of the people who'd tortured and sold him just so Matt could keep his daughter. Hopefully, they wouldn't need to have Tyler confront Pamela, but Tyler was ready to do it if he had to, and Matt could have kissed him for it.

Since he *could* kiss Tyler now, he did. Tyler's eyes widened when Matt reached for him, but he came easily, pressing against Matt's body. Tyler was short, but in Matt's arms, he felt perfect.

Matt had been underestimating Tyler since day one, and it was time to stop and rely on Tyler like he expected Tyler to rely on him. If they were going to be partners, *mates*, they needed to be there for each other and support each other. Right now, it was Matt who needed that support. Matt had to allow Tyler to provide it for him because Tyler thought he could, and Matt wanted to believe it. Hopefully, Tyler would tell him if it became too much. Matt would keep an eye on him to make sure Tyler was all right, but they had to face this like a family.

Because they were one.

Tyler could feel the moment Matt surrendered and accepted that they were supposed to support each other. If Matt needed anything, Tyler would be there for him, and if Tyler needed Matt, Matt wouldn't hesitate to support him. That was how mates worked and what Tyler had wanted all along.

"Thank you," Matt whispered.

"I'm here for you, now and for the future. I'm not going anywhere." And the sooner Matt accepted that, the sooner they could focus on building that future together.

Matt chuckled. "I'm starting to believe that. I guess I'm used to protecting my kids, but I have to let go of that way of thinking when it comes to you. You're not my child. You're my mate and an adult, and I need to trust that you know what you're doing. I can be there for you without treating you like a fragile child I need to protect."

Tyler pressed closer to Matt. "I do need you to protect me, but it's a two-sided road. I can protect you while you protect me."

"Yeah, you can."

For the first time, Tyler allowed himself to hope that everything would be okay. He didn't know if Pamela was Matt's ex-wife, but he'd find out eventually, and when he did, he and Matt would face it together. They were a family, and they'd stand up to Pamela as one.

"Let's go home," Matt said.

Tyler's chest felt tight. He had a home. He had a family.

And he'd do anything to keep both safe and never lose them.

They had to let go of each other, which Tyler wasn't happy about, but he wanted to go home. He needed to be in a comfortable setting because he could feel his skin itch with anxiety. He wasn't used to being out in the world. For the past couple of decades, his life had been in cages or luxurious homes. He'd never been allowed freedom, and now that he had it, it felt like almost too much. The world was too wide. Even pack territory felt too big, but Tyler wanted to get used to moving around it. Right now, though, home would be perfect.

They were silent as Matt drove them home. Tyler felt it was okay because even though they weren't talking, there was no tension between them. They'd found their way to each other, and while Tyler was sure it would take more work and that sometimes they would have a hard time living together, they were mates, and he had faith in their bond.

He wanted more. He wanted to be Matt's rock in the storm, to make him smile and laugh, to make him happy. Their future was together, and Tyler wanted everything he'd never had with Matt.

When Matt parked the car in front of the house, he didn't get out right away. Tyler waited with him, the feeling that Matt wanted to say something strong enough to make him not want to go into the house alone.

"The house is empty," Matt finally said.

"I'm aware."

Del was with Angus, while Cora was spending the afternoon and night with Doyle and Marcus. Marcus had been hesitant because, apparently, he didn't know what to do with a kid, but Cora had been excited at the thought of spending time with her brother. Everyone had thought it would be better for Matt to have the evening to breathe after the meeting with the lawyer.

Matt turned so he could look at Tyler. "We're in this together forever, right?"

"Of course."

"And I know you've been through a lot, and we don't have to do anything you're not ready for, especially since you didn't give me details about a lot of stuff, so I don't know what you might be comfortable with, but, well, I thought we could spend the night together."

Tyler found himself smiling. "Are you asking me if I want to have sex with you?"

Matt flushed and looked away. "Yeah, I guess. I feel like an idiot, but I haven't done this in a long time, and not with someone I love."

Tyler stared at him. Matt's cheeks flushed even harder, but he didn't take back his words. "You love me?" Tyler asked.

"Yeah. I'm in love with you, and I know those feelings will

become stronger in time. It's kind of scary, to be honest, because I already feel so strongly. I can't imagine how it'll be in a few years, but I want to find out."

Tyler beamed. "Let's go." He scrambled out of the car, eager to be in Matt's arms and in his bed. He'd never felt this way, and it was glorious. He never wanted it to end.

Matt laughed as he followed Tyler. Tyler was faster and made it upstairs before Matt could start up the stairs. As he went, he started shedding his clothes, leaving a trail for Matt to follow. He'd stopped feeling self-conscious a while ago since he spent so much time wearing next to nothing, but this was different. It was Matt, and Tyler knew he'd like what he'd see because he knew that he could. Whatever Matt looked like under his clothes, Tyler would love it.

Tyler threw himself onto the bed as soon as he was in Matt's room. He fought with his socks for a moment, then pushed his pants down his legs without taking them off. It was easier to do once his pants were off.

Matt stumbled into the room as Tyler dropped his underwear next to the bed.

And he stared.

Tyler stretched, exposing himself fully. Matt appeared frozen, and it made Tyler feel smug. It wasn't an emotion he was used to, but he didn't care that it felt odd. He just cared about Matt.

"You look like you belong in my bed," Matt croaked.

"That's because I do." Tyler had never been convinced of anything like he was convinced of that.

Matt nodded. Tyler continued watching him, and while he wasn't exactly elegant as he stripped, Tyler didn't need him to be.

He didn't know what to expect from Matt in bed. Matt was incredibly patient in his everyday life, not at all impulsive, and sweet and gentle. Tyler wasn't surprised to see it extended to how Matt was in bed. He should have known, really.

That didn't mean Matt wasn't passionate. If anything, his patience translated into driving Tyler nuts, first by taking ages to get naked and in bed, then by doing the same once their bodies were pressed together. He seemed to want to explore every inch of Tyler's body, which Tyler hadn't counted on, at least not for their first time. He'd imagined something slightly frantic, with both of them rushing toward pleasure. Getting to know each other physically could come later.

Matt didn't seem to feel the same way. He took his time, ignoring Tyler's requests for more. The only times he did listen to Tyler was when Tyler tried to get him to move to other places, but even then, he was tortuously slow. He paused at Tyler's nipples even though Tyler tried to push him down because his cock needed attention, and Tyler could feel him smile against his skin.

He huffed. "You're driving me nuts."

"Am I? I'm just exploring you."

"We can explore each other next time."

"Why rush? As you said, the house is empty, and it will be for hours."

"Which means we have time to do this again."

Matt laughed and kissed Tyler's belly button. Tyler pushed his hips up, groaning when the head of his cock pressed against Matt's chest. Was it too much to ask Matt to fuck him now?

"I just have a hard time believing you're really here," Matt murmured.

"I am, and I'm not going anywhere. Make this good for me, Matt. Make me yours." He wouldn't erase the memories, but Tyler didn't need him to. It was enough for them to create new ones.

Matt looked up at Tyler with eyes that burned with all the

love he felt. Tyler wanted to lose himself in them, but instead, he tilted his head toward the nightstand where there was a book and a bottle of water. "Lube?"

Matt stretched out to open the drawer. He rooted into it for a moment, then made a victorious sound and leaned back against Tyler. He had a tube of lube in his hand, and the sight made Tyler grin.

"Make me yours," Tyler repeated, opening his legs.

Matt obeyed.

Tyler had always known Matt would be good at this. He was a caretaker and enjoyed making the people he loved happy. Tyler was one of those people, and Matt was doing what he did best.

It didn't take long for him to have Tyler writhing on his fingers and begging for more. Matt had said he didn't have much experience, and maybe he didn't, but he certainly seemed to know what he was doing. He'd stretched out Tyler so well that when he slid his fingers out of Tyler's body, Tyler felt empty. Or maybe that was because Tyler desperately wanted his mate inside of him. Whatever the reason, Tyler was done waiting, and while Matt was careful as he positioned himself between Tyler's legs, Tyler could see how much he wanted him.

The time for slow and teasing was gone, and Matt was finally on board with that. He moved slowly but surely as he pushed into Tyler, and Tyler held his gaze. He needed to see that it was Matt inside him. He wasn't afraid and wanted this, but he was making the new memories he needed.

Tyler welcomed Matt inside his body and heart. Matt was giving him everything he'd ever wanted — love, happiness, a home, and a family.

Tyler wrapped his legs around Matt's hips and kept him close. Matt didn't give any hint he wanted to move away, thank god, but Tyler felt better clinging to him.

Matt pinned Tyler down and took him, and Tyler gave back as good as he got. They moved together like a couple because it was what they were. It didn't matter that they'd only been together a short time.

It was enough. It was *everything*.

CHAPTER SIX

M att watched, a smile playing on his lips. He couldn't have looked away even if he wanted to, and he didn't. Seeing Tyler and Cora cook together was a sight for sore eyes and something that made him incredibly happy.

Was this what he'd been missing all along? He'd kept his heart closed off because he hadn't wanted his attention to be taken away from his kids, but maybe, he could have had a partner who would have loved them as much as he did and who would have been with Cora since she was a baby.

Or maybe he wouldn't have found this with anyone but Tyler. They were mates, which Matt assumed had happened for a reason — maybe because Tyler had needed him that night after the auction, or maybe because Matt needed Tyler now. Whatever the reason, Matt couldn't imagine being with anyone else, no matter how recently he and Tyler had started dating.

But even though Tyler was a recent addition to his life, Matt couldn't deny that he already felt more stable. Sometimes, when he'd been on his own with three kids, he'd felt like he was drowning. Things had gotten easier as the boys grew up, but Matt still worried about them, especially after what Doyle had done. He'd never have imagined that his sweet-hearted son would kidnap someone, yet, Doyle had. It was a miracle that everything had ended up the way it had, rather than with Doyle behind bars or worse.

Matt had failed Doyle. Doyle had done what he'd done because the family had been desperate, and Matt would always feel guilty for that. But he had to look at their lives now. Doyle had met his mate and was happy with Marcus. The same had happened to Del, who was basically living with Angus. They hadn't made it official yet, but the nights Del spent with Angus came more often than the nights he spent in the house. He'd teased Matt, telling him it was because he wanted to give him and Tyler space, and maybe he did, but there was more to it. He was ready to spread his wings, and it gave Matt a little pang of pain. He'd known this would happen since Del was twenty, but it was still odd to think of the little boy who'd cuddled against his chest as a grown man who had a partner of his own.

And then, there was Cora. She'd always been a happy little girl, and Matt had done everything he could to make sure that didn't change. She'd blossomed under Tyler's attention, though. Something about Tyler spoke to her, and together, they were the best troublemakers. When Cora wasn't at school, at dance class, or with her friends, she was home with Tyler. They cooked, watched TV, and read together. Sometimes, Matt was worried it was too much for Tyler, who wasn't used to having a child around and hadn't asked for it, but Tyler seemed happy.

Just as much as Matt was.

There was so much that Matt stood to lose now that he was more scared than ever, especially with Pamela back in his life. He hadn't heard from her yet, but he had no doubt he would, and soon. The fact that she might be involved with the auctions made him want to call to yell at her, but he and Tyler had agreed it was better to keep their suspicions to themselves. Until Tyler knew for sure that Pamela was involved with the auctions and until she was out of their lives for good, they didn't want to make waves.

That was why Matt's stomach churned when Tyler's phone rang. He hadn't had it for long, and only a handful of people had his number. Cam did, as well as Preston, since he was working with them. Doyle and Del's numbers were in there, too, and Peregrine's, which had surprised Matt. He was glad Tyler was making friends. He wanted Tyler in his life and for them to be a family, but he couldn't be Tyler's entire life. He had to find out how much was out there waiting for him to explore and make friends. That was what he and Peregrine were doing.

Tyler patted Cora's shoulder, confirmed that she needed to continue stirring, and picked up his phone from the counter. He looked at the screen, then frowned and answered.

"Cam?"

Matt didn't know if he should relax or not. The alpha was calling, which could mean pretty much anything. Cam wasn't involved with the Pamela situation beyond knowing what was happening, so it probably wasn't that. Besides, he'd have called Matt himself if that had been the case.

Tyler looked up, and his gaze locked with Matt's.

"Yes, I can come over, but we have Cora at home, so I don't know if Matt can."

Whatever had happened, if Cam needed to see both Tyler and Matt, it couldn't be good. Matt sighed and took his phone out of his pocket, quickly texting the mother of Cora's best friend. The girls hadn't been supposed to see each other today since it was Sunday, but they'd be happy to spend a few hours together as long as it was okay with the parents.

Luckily, it was, and Cora rushed upstairs to pack a bag with toys and other things she wanted to show her friend. While she did that, Matt started cleaning up the kitchen. It didn't take Tyler long to hang up, and the kitchen was silent for a moment.

Matt had learned that if he wanted Tyler to talk to him, he needed to give him space. Tyler was used to being on his own and not being able to rely on anyone, very much like Matt. He had different reasons to behave that way, but it didn't change the fact that he didn't quite know how to rely on someone. Giving him time to realize that he could help.

"Cam wants to see us both," Tyler eventually said.

"I heard your side of the conversation. Did he say why?"

"Just that something happened."

"I suppose we'll find out soon enough." Matt kissed Tyler's cheek. "Why don't you go wash up? I'll make sure Cora is packed up, and we can go as soon as we drop her off."

Tyler hesitated, then nodded. He left the kitchen, giving Matt time to think everything through. He doubted Pamela was involved in whatever had happened since he hadn't heard from Preston, but there was something else Tyler was a part of. Angus and Everly had been looking for Pembroke since the auction, and Matt wondered if the summons had something to do with that.

It thrilled him to think that Tyler might be about to get his best friend back. He didn't want to get ahead of himself, but the hope was there, and he wasn't the only one to feel that way. When Tyler came back downstairs, he was almost vibrating with anticipation, and he didn't stop until they reached Cam's house after dropping off Cora.

Once they were there, Matt paused on the porch. Tyler leaned against him immediately as if it was natural for him to do so, and Matt smiled at the thought that it was becoming that way. They were still working to find their way around each other and how to be together, but their foundation was solid. Whatever happened outside of their relationship wouldn't hurt them. They'd face it together, and while it was a somewhat odd feeling, it was also something that Matt didn't want to go without now that he had it.

He kissed the top of Tyler's head. "Everything will be all right," he promised.

"As long as we're together," Tyler added.

"As long as we're together," Matt confirmed.

And he truly believed that.

Tyler didn't know why Cam wanted to see him any more than Matt did, but he wasn't worried. So far, Cam hadn't given him any reason not to trust him and the pack, and he hoped things stayed that way. He'd finally found a home, and he wasn't going to lose it just because he was afraid.

And he was. It would be easy to obsess over whatever was about to happen, to start making up scenarios and worry, but Tyler refused to. He was safe, dammit, and that wasn't going to change just because the alpha wanted to talk to him.

He and Matt headed there, sticking together as promised. Tyler wouldn't have it any other way, and he was glad to have Matt by his side. Matt was the one person Tyler wanted with him if something had happened. They were in a good place, and Tyler hoped that wasn't about to change. He also hoped that whatever Cam needed from him, it didn't have anything to do with Matt. Tyler hadn't met Pamela yet, and he wasn't planning on seeing her anytime soon, but he'd face her if it meant protecting his family. He'd been on his own for too long. Now that he had someone to fight for, he wouldn't hesitate — bad memories and nightmares be damned.

Like everything in pack territory, Cam's house wasn't far. The weather was nice since it was summer, but Tyler wasn't able to enjoy it. He was focused on what was about to happen and knowing himself, that wouldn't change until he found out what it was. Thankfully, they were there, and the door swung open as soon as they knocked.

Toby waved them in. "Everyone's in the office."

He guided them there even though they knew where it was. He didn't leave, clearly intending to be here for this meeting. Tyler liked that. Even though Cam was the alpha, he and Toby were a team, very much like Matt and Tyler.

Tyler had suspected who else would be there when Toby mentioned that everyone was in the office, so he wasn't surprised to see Angus and Everly sitting on the couch, both typing away on their computers. Angus looked up when he heard Matt and Tyler, and his smile made Tyler feel better. It was odd to think he and Angus were family. Tyler had gained much more than just Matt when he and Matt had decided to be together. Angus was part of that much more and seemed to have good news.

"I think I have enough for us to be able to go in and get Pembroke back," Angus explained, looking around the room.

Tyler's eyes widened, and he let go of Matt's hand to move closer. "How is he? Do you know?"

"Not really. I've been keeping an eye on Colbert's phone, but he doesn't talk about the shifters he owns. He knows better, I guess, which is a bit of a problem, but it doesn't mean we won't be able to go in. I have his security app, which means I can access the entire house. I don't know if he's stupid or if he thought no one would hack his phone just because he's rich, but he should have been more careful regarding security."

"Don't give bad guys ideas," Everly muttered. He glanced up and grinned at Tyler. "But Angus is right. Colbert thought he was out of reach and wasn't careful with his phone. You might not be aware of that since you only got a phone recently, but most people have their entire lives on their phones. Colbert isn't any different. I could take away all his money with just a few strokes of my keyboard."

Tyler was tempted to tell him to do just that, but it wasn't his place. Besides, he just wanted Pembroke back. He didn't care about Colbert, although he wouldn't mind seeing him punished for what he'd done.

Tyler had known him for years. He was Fulton's best

friend, which was probably how he'd managed to get his hands on Pembroke. He'd paid a lot for Pem, but everyone had known he wanted him and that he was Fulton's friend. They'd given him a wide berth and had allowed him to win the auction, and he'd taken Pembroke home with him.

And now, it looked like he was about to lose him.

"Tell us what you know," Cam said.

Tyler was grateful for the interruption, because he didn't know where to start. He wanted to go out there and get Pembroke back right away, but it was nothing more than a dream. They'd have to plan and go around security—and not just cameras. If Colbert wasn't a complete idiot, he'd have a small army of shifters protecting his home. Even though he wouldn't hurt a fly, Pembroke was probably one of those shifters. He might be a hydra shifter, but that didn't mean he was violent or cruel.

No, that was Colbert and his friends.

"Maybe you should call Ryland before I start," Angus pointed out. "He's going to be pissed we didn't involve him otherwise, and he knows something's happening since I texted him."

Cam rolled his eyes but reached for his phone. Tyler knew that Ryland was paying for most of the things he'd been using since he'd arrived here. Tyler was a pack member now, and not just because he was with Matt. Cam had asked him if he wanted to be one, and he'd said yes. That meant the pack was responsible for him until he could contribute to pack life, and while he was eager to start, he was also terrified because he had no idea how to do any of this. He'd lived on the streets for a few years before being taken and auctioned. He'd never had a normal life, and he'd never had a job. He was thankful to Ryland for paying his way with the pack, and to the pack for supporting him. Hopefully, he'd one day be able to pay that debt, even though he knew they wouldn't see it that way.

How they saw it didn't matter. It *was* a debt, and Tyler didn't like feeling like he owed them so much.

But for now, he had other things to focus on and every intention of doing just that. Pembroke needed him.

"Anything new?" Ryland asked when he answered.

"Hello to you, too."

"Yes, hello. Now tell me."

"We have news," Cam admitted. "I don't know what news yet because Angus insisted we call you before saying anything."

"I knew he was my favorite for a reason."

Cam grinned. "I have no doubt. Are you ready to listen?"

"I am. Talk to us, Angus."

Angus nodded. "As I was saying, I had enough time with Colbert's phone. I know what his security system looks like and how we can get around it. I'm not sure where Pembroke is located, so that's something we'll have to deal with once we're there, but I found his name in the list of house security personnel, so I'm pretty sure Colbert is using him as a guard."

"It would make sense, considering what he can shift into," Cam offered.

"I suppose. How fierce is Pembroke?" Angus asked, looking at Tyler.

Tyler snorted. "Pembroke isn't a violent person. He'd rather die than to hurt someone, which I'm sure was a disappointment when Colbert found out."

"He might have found a way to force my brother to work with him," Ryland said in a grim voice.

Tyler's stomach churned. He remembered all too well the kind of treatment he and the other shifters who'd been auctioned had gone through. Tyler had seen horrors he hoped he'd never see again, and he'd lived through them. He needed his best friend to be okay.

"Whatever happened to Pembroke, we need to go there as

soon as possible," Cam said. "We have the layout of the house, and we'll be able to find Pembroke easily enough as long as Angus keeps an eye on Colbert's security system. He and Everly will be able to guide us through the house to get us to Pembroke, so hopefully, we won't have too much of a fight on our hands." Cam looked at Tyler. "Will you be going along?"

Tyler blinked. He hadn't expected that question and wasn't sure how to answer. He wanted to say yes because he needed his best friend back in his life, but would he be of any use?

He looked at Matt, wanting his opinion. He half expected Matt to tell him not to go. His mate was fiercely protective of him, which made sense. Everyone in the room knew Tyler's history, so they wouldn't blame him for wanting to stay back.

"You think I should go?" he asked Matt.

"I think you should do whatever you feel comfortable doing. I also think that Pembroke will be happy to see you, though. Maybe you could shift into your gargoyle form? It's sturdy enough that you shouldn't be hurt even if someone attacks you, right?"

Tyler squared his shoulders and nodded. "I'll be fine as long as I'm in that form. I should stay back, though. I need to protect you and Cora."

"We'll be fine."

"They can both stay here with Toby and me during the mission," Cam said. "But I think Matt is right. You should be there for Pembroke."

Tyler sucked in a breath. "Then I will be."

Matt understood why Tyler was wary of leaving him and Cora behind. He'd taken his role as a protector quite seriously, and maybe, he wasn't wrong to do so. Pamela had gotten into pack territory once, after all. No one had realized she'd come in, and while Cam had asked people to keep an eye out, it wasn't like pack territory was surrounded by fences or gated. People were free to come and go, and while most humans who lived in the small town next to the pack knew better than to stick their noses into pack territory without reason, pack members were so used to not see anyone strange that they weren't quite sure what to look out for.

But the twins had promised to keep an eye open, and Matt had seen them train. Lennox was silent and lethal, and if Pamela tried anything, she'd be dealt with. Lennox's twin was a lot more chatty—enough for both of them—but no less dangerous. If anything, Matt was pretty sure he'd seen him bounce on his feet at the thought of beating someone up, which had scared him a bit, even though he was glad he and Cora were under Carey's protection.

They'd be fine. They had to be, and by the time this was over, Tyler's best friend would be with them, or at the very least, he'd be free. No one knew if Pembroke would decide to go back with his brother or stick around with the pack, but at the moment, it didn't matter. They'd have time to find out what Pembroke wanted once he was free and with them. First, they needed to get to him.

"When are we leaving?" Ryland asked.

Matt could hear him talk to someone who wasn't on the phone with them, then the sound of him moving. Matt had no doubt he was already headed here and that he'd be there as quickly as the speed limits allowed him to.

Cam took a moment to answer. "We should be ready once you're here. When we hang up, I'll start calling people. We'll need support to get in and out, and I know a few people who would be happy to come along. I can't come along, unfortunately."

"I didn't expect you to, and I understand that decision. It doesn't matter. I want my brother back, and I'll take anyone on with my bare hands if it means Pembroke is safe."

Matt had no doubt Ryland would do just that. The two of them shared that. They might be human, but they wouldn't hesitate to take on someone, even a shifter if it meant keeping the people they loved safe.

"I don't think things will come to that," Cam reassured Ryland. "I have a few people in mind. I don't think we need more if Angus and Everly can work on the security system from here. It would be better for us to sneak in and out of the property rather than attack it head-on. We want to be discreet, not burn it to the ground."

Matt wasn't quite sure about that. Colbert hadn't bought Tyler, but Tyler had explained he was friends with Fulton, which made him one of the bad guys. Matt wouldn't hesitate to punch him if he could, and he thought that maybe, someone should make sure Colbert couldn't continue buying shifters. He wouldn't be able to if someone took away all his money and his home.

But that wasn't Matt's decision, and he had nothing to add to the situation. He wouldn't be going along to get Pembroke. He'd stay back and hold down the fort, and when Tyler came home, he'd be there, waiting with open arms.

That was what Tyler needed. He needed to feel loved and to know he wasn't alone, and Matt was happy to give him that.

Tyler leaned against Matt's side, and Matt curled an arm around his shoulders. He kissed the top of his head, wondering how to manage the anxiety. He wouldn't stop Tyler from going on the mission, and he couldn't go with him, but he'd be worried. What if something happened to Tyler? Matt would be too far to help him, although he doubted he'd be able to do anything even if he was there. He was only human, and it sounded like Colbert had a security system made up of shifters. Matt would probably be more of a hindrance than anything if he went on this rescue mission. So, instead, he'd freak out and worry from afar.

He had to let Tyler spread his wings. Tyler might look fragile, and he was small, but there was a heart of stone beating in his chest. He was a gargoyle, and Matt had seen what he turned into when he shifted. No one would be able to hurt him as long as he stayed in that form, and Matt had every intention of asking him to do just that. He couldn't forbid Tyler to go, and he wouldn't have wanted to even if he could, but he could ask for that. He needed Tyler to be safe.

"Matt, why don't you call one of your sons and have them pick up Cora from school?" Cam suggested. "They could all come here."

It was a surprise to hear that things would go that fast after they'd had to wait so long, but Matt was on board. He could only imagine what was happening to Pembroke, and he wanted him out as much as everyone else. He didn't care that he'd never met the guy. His being Tyler's best friend was enough.

He stepped away and texted both Del and Doyle at the same time using their group chat. Del was on it immediately, and while it took Doyle a moment longer to answer, he was on board, too. Things wouldn't be easy for Matt over the next few hours, but he wouldn't face this on his own.

He kissed the top of Tyler's head again. "I'm going to head home," he said. "I'll pick up a few things for Cora and be right back. Del is picking her up, and he'll bring her straight here."

"I'll come with you," Tyler said, already moving.

Matt shook his head. "You need to stay here and listen to what Angus found. You're going on this mission and need all the information you can get. I need you to be safe."

"We all do," Cam confirmed. "Besides, Matt will be right back, right?"

"I wouldn't want to be anywhere else," Matt promised.

"I'll come with you," Tyler insisted.

Matt could see he wouldn't change Tyler's mind, so he nodded. If this was what Tyler needed to feel secure, Matt would give it to him.

"We'll be back in about half an hour, probably less," he told the alpha. "If anything happens, call us."

"It'll take Ryland that time to get here, but I'm sure he'll want to move as soon as he arrives. As long as you're here by then, I don't have a problem with the two of you leaving. If you want to be involved in this mission, Tyler, you need to be back by the time Ryland arrives."

"I will be," Tyler promised.

Matt would do anything he could to make sure that happened. This was important to Tyler, which meant it was important to Matt.

The two of them left Cam's house and headed back home. Matt could feel Tyler almost vibrating with anxiousness and excitement, and it made him smile. In the beginning, he'd thought Tyler was soft and gentle, and most of the time, he was. There was a great strength in him, though, and he was ready to put it to work. If he had to free Pembroke on his own, he would.

But it was good to know he wouldn't be alone.

As soon as they were home, they headed upstairs. Matt didn't think they'd have to stay with Cam and Toby for long, so he didn't pack an overnight bag for himself, but he did grab a change of clothes for Cora and some of her toys. She'd need to be entertained while they waited, and Matt wasn't sure he'd be in the right mind to do that, so he also took his tablet. A bit of screen time wouldn't hurt her, and it would allow Matt and the others to focus on the rescue mission.

Del had texted Matt to tell him he'd gotten Cora and was headed to Cam's house, so Matt was surprised to hear a knock on the front door. He and Tyler looked at each other, but when Tyler moved to go open, Matt shook his head.

"I'll go. Finish packing Cora's stuff, all right? Maybe add some pajamas. If the mission goes on late, she might fall asleep."

Tyler didn't look convinced but nodded, and Matt headed downstairs.

He knew he'd been right to tell Tyler to stay upstairs when he opened the door and found Pamela waiting for him on the porch.

Tyler's instincts were screaming at him that something was about to happen, but he tried to convince himself it had to do with the rescue mission. Still, he kept an ear open so he could listen to Matt talk to whoever was at the door, and he tensed when he realized it was a woman. Tyler didn't want to believe Pamela was back, but who else could it be? Any other woman in Tyler and Matt's lives would have called instead of coming straight to their home. There was only one woman who would have knocked on the door, probably in the hope of finding them with Cora.

Tyler was done with this. He needed to focus on Pembroke, but he wouldn't be able to if he knew Pamela was hanging around and scaring Matt. Tyler was terrified of her, even though she'd never physically hurt him, but it was time to face that fear. Once he had, he'd be able to go out, get Pembroke back, and focus on the people he loved.

"Where is my daughter?" the woman asked loud enough that Tyler heard her.

He straightened his shoulders, ready to fight. He moved toward the stairs, his stomach churning and making him feel like he was about to throw up. Maybe he'd do so in Pamela's face. That wouldn't be such a bad thing.

"She's not here," Matt was saying. He was keeping his

voice calm, but Tyler could hear the turmoil in his tone.

"You're keeping her from me," Pamela accused. "You can't continue doing that, Matt. I'm her mother, and you're nothing to her."

"I'm her father, and I know enough to be aware of the fact that she's at school. That's probably something you should know if you want to be in her life."

There was a pause, but Tyler knew Pamela wouldn't be cowed. It wasn't the kind of person she was.

He hesitated once he reached the top of the stairs, but Matt needed him, and he'd promised to be there for him when that happened. He told himself he was ready. He didn't know if it was true, but he was about to find out.

"I'll wait here until she comes back from school," Pamela declared.

Tyler quickly took out his phone and texted Cam to let him know what was happening. Pamela's presence in pack territory while they were organizing a raid on Colbert's home could only be a coincidence, but it made Tyler uneasy. The only people who knew what was happening had only known for a short time, too short for any of them to call Pamela and have her come here to spy on them. Besides, Tyler trusted all of them with his life and Pembroke's. Pamela was here to start trouble, but she didn't know, which meant they had to get rid of her.

Tyler was done packing Cora's things and brought the bag downstairs. Matt couldn't see him because he had his back to him, but Pamela glanced up when she heard him. Her eyes widened, then narrowed. Tyler glared at her, wondering how she'd want to do this.

"Tyler," she said, glaring right back at him.

"You need to leave," Tyler told her.

She arched a brow. "Do I? I'm here for my daughter."

"You don't have a daughter. You don't care about her

because you can't care about anyone. Everyone says that I have a heart of stone because I'm a gargoyle shifter, but it's nothing compared to yours. Your heart is made of ice, and not one part of you cares about your kids." Tyler faced her, letting the words flow out of his mouth. "But I do. She already had Matt, and she has me now, too. We won't allow you to hurt her, and I know exactly the kind of person you are. You'll never lay a hand on her."

Pamela's gaze flickered to Matt. "I suppose you told him?"

"I know everything," Matt said. "And I need you to leave. I wouldn't allow you to see Cora even if you were the last person alive on earth. I always knew you were selfish, but I didn't realize how evil you'd become."

She crossed her arms over her chest. "You won't be able to prove anything. No one would believe *him*." She jerked her chin toward Tyler.

"Maybe, maybe not, but you didn't count on one thing."

Pamela huffed. "I thought of everything. I always do."

Usually, that was true, but she'd underestimated Matt. Tyler loved to see it, and he loved to watch Matt stand up to her. They knew for sure that she was the same person who would hurt Tyler now, which meant there was no way Matt would allow her anywhere close to his family ever again.

"I'm not alone anymore," Matt said, his voice calm and strong. He wasn't yelling, but he didn't need to.

She snorted. "Are you telling me you and Tyler are together? Please. He might be a gargoyle shifter, but he's never hurt anyone. He's not capable of it."

"He might not be, but what about the rest of the pack? The rest of *my* pack? Because it's not just the kids and me anymore. Del and Doyle both have shifter mates. We have a pack, a place where we belong, and people who will fight for us. Some of them won't hesitate to make you disappear without a trace, and while I never want to be the kind of person who makes that decision, I will if it means protecting my family."

Pamela stared. She looked shocked, which Tyler was delighted to see. He stood next to Matt, pressing a hand against his back to silently remind him that he wasn't alone.

There was the pack and Tyler, who wouldn't hesitate to shift and tear Pamela apart if it meant keeping Matt safe. That wasn't something Pamela had counted on, and she was clearly trying to find a way out of the situation.

She hadn't thought of everything this time.

"You wouldn't let anyone hurt me," she eventually said.

"I wouldn't push it if I were you," Matt warned. "You know I'd do anything to protect my family, and that includes getting rid of you. I wouldn't even care how they do it."

"I'm not alone. I have a lot of people and a lot of money, and I want my daughter back. That means I'll get her."

"Never. She has people who will protect her now, and as far as going the legal way, I've already found a lawyer. Considering the fact that you abandoned both your daughter and your sons, renounced your parental rights to all three of them, and agreed to have me adopt her, he says you don't stand a chance in hell of getting Cora back. We can certainly fight it out if you want." Matt leaned closer. "But I'd think twice about it if I were you. I know what you are, and I'm sure you know the kind of people I have on my side. Do you really want to go against them?"

Pamela looked pissed, which was lovely to see. Tyler wanted to poke at her again, but he knew how she could become when she got angry. He wouldn't put anything past her. He didn't think she wanted Cora back, but she wouldn't hesitate to take her if she had the opportunity to do so, even if it was only to spite Matt.

"You'll regret this," she spat out. "You won't have anything left when I'm done with you—not your daughter, not your pack, not Tyler." She smiled, beautiful and evil. "You don't know who you're going against."

"I think I do," Matt said, stepping forward so she had to move back. "I'm going against a bunch of people who think they can hurt shifters without repercussions. I'm going against a woman who is so selfish that she wouldn't hesitate to take her daughter from the only home and parent she's ever known. I don't know why you're here or what you thought to obtain by trying to get back into our lives, but I won't allow you to hurt anyone again. It's not only the kids. The pack is my home, and I'll protect it from you and anyone else on your side."

"You can certainly try, but we'll win. We always do."

Tyler had had enough. He grabbed Matt and pulled him back into the house, then slammed the door shut in Pamela's face. He wished he could see her expression but wasn't about to open it again. He wanted her out, so he leaned against the door, listening to her as she left.

"This is a fucking mess," Matt said, running his hands through his hair.

"It is, but it's a mess we'll face together," Tyler promised.

CHAPTER SEVEN

Tyler was nervous. He wanted to be here, but he'd never been a fighter, even though he was a gargoyle shifter. He was afraid to mess up everything, and he'd already decided to stay back for as long as he could. The only moment he wouldn't was when they found Pembroke, and that was more because he didn't think he'd be able to stay back. Pembroke would need him, and they hadn't seen each other in too long. He wouldn't be able to keep his cool once he finally got his best friend back.

"You shouldn't be here," Ryland bitched next to Tyler. "It's too dangerous, and my brother would never forgive me if something happened to his best friend."

"He doesn't want anything to happen to you, either," Tyler pointed out.

Ryland jerked back a little as if he hadn't expected the sound of Tyler's voice. Maybe he hadn't. Tyler's gargoyle voice was so different from his voice in his human form that most people were startled when they talked to him. It was kind of fun to watch, to be honest.

"Nothing will happen to anyone," Mercer grumbled.

Tyler had expected more people to come, so he'd been surprised when he saw there would be only a handful of them. Ryland wouldn't have been left behind, and of course, Remi was with him. Cam had also sent a few of his guards along, including his brother, Bryson. All in all, Tyler felt protected but also awkward.

He'd been ordered to stay back and was perfectly fine with

it. The people who knew what they were doing had the lead, and if they needed him to intervene, he wouldn't hesitate, but he was fine not giving orders. Ryland clearly didn't feel the same way. He was nervous and kept bitching that they needed to go in, and the only reason he hadn't run into danger on his own, leaving all of them behind, was that Remi had glared at him and Mercer had slapped the back of his head the one time he'd tried.

Tyler had been impressed. Even though Ryland was human, there was an air of power and authority to him that would have stopped him from even thinking about slapping him. Mercer didn't have that problem and seemingly didn't care that Ryland was still glaring at him.

The sound of someone clearing their throat made Tyler jump before he realized it came from the earbud in his ear. All of them had one, and through them, they could hear Angus and Everly. The two of them had hooked into the security system, which meant they had access to all the cameras and their feed. They knew where everyone in the house was, which Tyler and the others would need, considering how big the place was.

Tyler wasn't impressed. He'd lived in houses with dozens of bedrooms and gold-plated toilets. He'd hated it and preferred his small house in pack territory.

"One of the guards is about to walk past you," Angus said. "Wait until he's gone, then move ahead. He's doing rounds, which means he won't be back in this area for another ten minutes."

The tension rocketed, and he got himself ready. He could hear the guard coming closer and see him from where he and the others were hiding in the bushes.

He'd felt ridiculous initially. After climbing the wall around the property, they'd hidden and waited for Angus and Everly to give them the go-ahead. That was when Ryland had almost done the stupidest thing he could have done and had attempted to go in on his own. Thankfully, Mercer and Remi had stopped him, and everyone was in one piece.

For the moment.

"Go," Angus ordered.

Everyone moved. Tyler and Ryland stayed behind the others, bracketed by Mercer and Remi. Tyler was careful of his wings because he didn't want anyone to trip on them, but unfortunately, in this form, he wasn't quite as inconspicuous as he usually was. He would have had an easier time hiding if he were in his human form, but this was the compromise he and Matt had agreed on. Matt knew he was safe as long as he was in his gargoyle form. Tyler's skin meant that no one could hurt him in any way, for which Tyler was glad. He was ready to use his form to protect the others, even though they probably thought they didn't need it.

Following Angus's directions, they managed to reach the mansion. They paused, hiding behind some trees as another guard walked past them. This one was on his phone, bickering with a woman with a loud voice who had to be his girlfriend or wife. He didn't notice them, even though it was pretty much impossible to miss Tyler, even hiding behind a pine tree.

"Once you round the corner, you'll find yourself in a courtyard," Angus said. "There's something in the courtyard that's moving, but I can't quite see what it is. You need to be careful."

As if they hadn't been until now. Tyler didn't say it out loud, but he thought it. Angus was doing what he could, like everyone else. They all needed Pembroke to come back to them in one piece and for everyone involved to be safe.

"Now," Angus said.

They moved.

Tyler didn't care about what was waiting for them in the

courtyard. He just cared about getting to Pembroke, but he still allowed the others to move ahead of him. He'd know what they found as soon as they saw it, and if it was an enemy, they'd be able to protect him.

Tyler didn't know who else it could be since they were behind enemy lines.

They burst into the courtyard. Tyler quickly looked around, but something ahead of them moved before he could make sense of what he was seeing and try to find a way to get into the house. It was massive, and for a moment, Tyler stared, his mouth dropping open.

He hadn't seen Pembroke in his hydra form often because it was massive. Pembroke had been forbidden to shift while they were still at the auction house, and it had weighed heavily on him. It had also been better that way because it meant he couldn't be used, but not shifting was hard for a shifter.

Pembroke clearly didn't have the same problem here. He was in his hydra form, standing tall in front of them, ready to protect Colbert's home. He rose high above his legs, stomping one foot, then the other, making the ground shake under them. His three heads moved, lowering to get a better reach as he opened his mouths.

"He's going to eat us," someone muttered.

Ryland tried jostling forward, but Tyler pushed past him. He didn't know what state of mind Pembroke was in, but he'd never forgive himself if he hurt his brother. Ryland was human and breakable, soft in all the wrong places. Tyler had no such problem and placed himself in front of the group, not afraid anymore.

The others would have his back when it came to the guards and Colbert.

He flared his wings open, grinning at the way Pembroke suddenly stopped moving.

"Are we even sure it's him?" Bryson asked.

For a moment, Tyler wondered if Colbert could possibly have two hydra shifters. Luckily, he didn't have to wonder for long because the hydra in front of him shuddered, then started shifting back.

Into Pembroke.

Tyler stayed in his gargoyle form, even though he felt awkward. As soon as Pembroke was in his human form, he threw himself at Tyler, and Tyler was careful as he wrapped his stone arms around his best friend. He didn't want to crush him or hurt him in any way.

"You're safe now," he whispered.

"I didn't think I'd see you ever again," Pembroke said with a sob.

He was naked, but no one cared. They only cared about taking him away before someone noticed what was happening.

Tyler leaned down and hauled Pembroke into his arms. He turned to face the others, not caring that they looked shocked or that Ryland appeared like he wanted to jump into Tyler's arms right along with Pembroke.

"Get us out of here," Tyler said, his voice strong and steady.

Mercer and Remi moved right away, going back from where they'd come from. Tyler could hear Angus talk into his ear, but his entire focus was on Pembroke, who'd snuggled against his chest. He didn't look afraid. He looked like he trusted Tyler to keep him safe, and Tyler promised himself he'd do just that.

"You're safe now," he told his friend.

Pembroke opened his eyes and looked up at him. "I know."

ABOUT THE AUTHOR

Catherine is the creator of several series, most of them paranormal, including the Whitedell Pride Series and the Gillham Pack Series. While she graduated in translation, she decided to go the writer's way because it was more fun to create her own stories and characters.

She's been living in Italy for more than twenty years, but she's a daughter of the North—Belgium to be precise—and she misses it so much that she's already planning to move back.

She loves pizza—probably too much—her son, her pets, and of course, books. She sneaks some reading time into her schedule every time she has five minutes free from writing, demands from her various pets and son, and lastly, housework.

Connect with her:

lievens.catherine@gmail.com
BookBub: https://www.bookbub.com/authors/catherine-lievens
Website: https://authorcatherinelievens.com/
Facebook: https://www.facebook.com/catherine.lievens.9
Facebook Group: https://www.facebook.com/groups/411788002341528/
Twitter: https://twitter.com/authorCLievens
Newsletter: http://eepurl.com/c-uvKn

www.ingramcontent.com/pod-product-compliance
Lightning Source LLC
Chambersburg PA
CBHW071627140626
46555CB00021B/878